Maz and Me

Sharon Loveday

Through The Door Publications

To Cymone
Enjoy!
Sharon Loveday

I dedicate this book to my family and friends

Maz and Me is my debut comic novel following a late start in gaining a Bachelor of Arts Degree in Creative Writing and Literature and a separate Diploma in Creative Writing. I regularly visit the Hay Festival of Literature and part of this book has been inspired by those visits.

'I don't watch television, I think it destroys the art of talking about oneself.'
Stephen Fry

CHAPTER ONE

'You can't take cannabis to Paris,' Maz says, and I notice a shadow of worry playing on her brow.

'It's only a little stash in the bottom of my rucksack, so no-one's going to find it. Anyway, it's for relaxation at bedtime in the hotel. I'm doing without porn aren't I? Ooh, I am wondering if I can manage four days without it.' I say that about the porn, using sarcasm, to wind her up just like I did when I was a teenager. Sometimes I find myself slipping back in to that teen mode, and can't seem to help it no matter how many times I try to convince myself of my manhood. Usually, she just shrugs when I do the sarcasm thing and never rises to the bait or retaliates, just leaves me to feel bad about it.

Although I'm thirty I've never been to Paris, or anywhere else for that matter, and was pleased when Maz asked if I wanted to go. I thought it would be good to reacquaint with some of the French buddies I made, when they stayed as students many summers in her house. When I agreed to go, I thought it would be just Maz and me. I didn't realise she was taking Jolly John the copper with us.

'The hotel has an entire no-smoking policy, and you know we've got John coming with us. He's ex-police. Not only ex-police, but ex Met detective,' she says, putting emphasis on the 'Met detective' bit, and I notice her hand slightly shaking on the knife as she slices through the bread for our sandwiches.

'So you think he can smell out dope like a bloodhound? Perhaps he's so good, he can detect it at two hundred metres,' I say. Maybe it's because I am still annoyed that the copper is coming with us, or because she told me not to bring the dope like it was a statement of fact, that I can't help the scornful reply, but I am aware I have seriously worried her.

'You really are being caustic now, Tony. I just want this trip to go well, and I think you'll enjoy it, so please leave the cannabis at home.'

'There are windows at the hotel, aren't there? I can blow the smoke in to the night air?'

'You might set off a fire alarm.'

'I promise, you can be more worried about me leaning too far out of the window than setting off any fire alarm,' I retort, like I'm unconcerned. Actually, I am a bit concerned that she will change her mind about me accompanying her if I keep up the mindless argument. Recently, I've been bothered about why I have this compulsion to be sarcastic. I have been reading a lot about Humanism, in the past few months, and making mental notes to try harder at adopting qualities of kindness and rationality. I actually care a lot about Maz. She listens if you need to talk over a problem and you can have a good conversation with her.

I've been visiting her house for fifteen years since her son brought me home after school one day, when we were in year ten. After dinner, he quickly got bored with me, and went outside to ride his BMX. I stayed in with his mum, following her round the house trying to keep up a stream of conversation, to which she listened intently and replied appropriately. She didn't seem bad-looking to a fifteen-year-old boy, but now as a thirty-year-old man, I find her to be a bit of a turn-on if I'm honest. Anyway, you should've seen my mate's sister. He kept it quiet that he had this gorgeous sister only a year older than us who went to a different school. Once we found out about her, there were loads of us lads aged about fifteen, going to his house on some pretext or other, fancying the fascinating sexy sixteen-year-old girl.

7

She used to drive us mad when she brought a rug out into the garden, and sat or lay down, dressed in shorts, surrounded by her school books. I remember her fingers were stained with ink, and she was totally oblivious to us while she concentrated on her study. The others used to leap about like inept idiots, trying to impress her with their antics, but she hardly ever looked up. I took a more subtle approach, acting as a fifteen-year-old philosopher full of mystery. I used to press my thumb under my chin, and produce a frown between my eyes, as I nodded with deep thought at everything she ever said. That approach was a dismal disaster too, and it just gave me permanently ingrained deep lines in my brow for which most people might have taken a shot of Botox by now.

'You're like bees round a honeypot,' an old man called over the fence as he took a surreptitious gander at her long legs.

'No, we're like flies round a turd,' my mate Cheddar shouted back, which I thought was pretty witty at the time but, with hindsight, realise it was a typical cruel Cheddar comment. Then, of course, he could be relied on for his brutal comments and witticisms. I remember when we were in year nine and our teacher set a piece of homework where we each had to research the meaning of another student's name. Unfortunately for me, it was Cheddar who was given the task of looking up the meaning of my name. The next day, when it was his turn to present his meaning, and source of research, I just knew something awful was about to happen. It was all in his stance. Standing tall, he swept his head from side to side, to make sure he had full audience attention, and there was this smirk on his face that only Cheddar can produce. He made his announcement in a more than usually powerful voice.

'*Tony*, as his name is not shortened from Antony, means "*simpleton*" as sourced from the Chambers Dictionary.' He put massive emphasis on 'simpleton', then he milked the merriment he caused by giving subtle head bows, with his hand behind his back, until the class of, 'Princesses, Handsomes, Mercifuls and

Man Warriors' had stopped laughing. I swear that moment caused me some post-traumatic stress.

Maz, who prefers to be called Maz rather than her given name of Marion, interrupts my musings by ripping across some foil to wrap the sandwiches.

'You know Maz, you did a good job of being a mother. You should do what you want with your life now your kids have left home. No-one's going to judge you.' I am trying to loosen her up a little, by giving it a bit of largesse, because she's obviously worried about my stash. It's not like I'm an addict, I just like a smoke at night to unwind, to help with sleep, and cigarettes don't do it for me. I have put a tiny amount in plastic then wrapped it in foil, so it looks like a piece of discarded chewing gum in the bottom fold of my rucksack. The mystical idea that you're protected from bad luck, by always following rules, bores me. We shouldn't have to worry so much about everything. I was a teenager who believed that if I checked the taps with a double turn, and made sure the towel was folded properly, edge to edge, I could prevent harm coming to anybody. As an adult, I have used my brain, applied logic, and have concluded that although I have superior brain power to most other humans, I am not that 'supremely all powerful'. The folding of a towel, or some other obsessive action like sticking to every rule that is ever presented, will not determine someone else's future. Anyway, it got boring.

I haven't been very kind to Maz, by winding her up, so I make a mental note to start working on my problem use of sarcasm. I wish I could speak easily to women my own age like I usually do with Maz. Mostly, I think women of my age are intimidated by my brainpower, but I'd just like a fraction of some action on the sex front. My mission on this trip is to get laid, or at least find a girlfriend.

CHAPTER TWO

At St Pancras we meet her mate, the 'ex Met' retired copper. I met him a few times before, and we got on okay. I wouldn't go so far as to say we liked each other, but he had some interesting stories to tell. In my head, I nicknamed him 'The Smiling Assassin' because he'll be grinning while he knocks you down with his opinions. Like the time I said, 'It's a free world, we shouldn't have a border control' and he went ballistic, barking his opinions at me. He's one of those perfectionist types with creases ironed down the front of his trousers, so sharp they look like you could use them to give yourself a close shave.

'Tony, nice to see you again,' he offers his hand. I shake his hand loosely, and realise, that for Maz's sake, I must do my best to tolerate him during our trip. They've both brought bloody great suitcases to lug around, and it's hard to imagine what they needed to bring for only four days.

'How did you get everything into that little rucksack? I envy that, being able to travel light,' Maz says, as she grabs my arm, pulling me to one side, while John fumbles for his passport. She whispers sternly, 'Go through Customs on your own if you've got what you threatened to bring, I don't want him associated with anything if you get stopped.' Then she trots across to John, takes his arm, and nods at me to go on without them.

As I dump my bag on the conveyor belt, I watch as Maz allows the people behind her in the queue to go ahead of her and

John, by putting on a pretext of having to adjust her shoe. Jovial John doesn't seem to notice anything unusual as he is eyeing up the women in the queue next to ours, trying to attract attention by beaming at them. By the time Maz and John pass the baggage check, I am safely the other side, and flick my ponytail in triumph. The top of my head's a bit bald, and annoyingly shiny, so I tried to draw attention away from it by growing a ponytail.

Before being called to board the Eurostar, we passed an hour in the waiting lounge at St Pancras. Once we were in the coffee bar, Maz and John grabbed the clean chairs, leaving me the one with a big brown stain, which looked suspiciously like someone, had had more than a slight accident, or spilt their coffee. It took some deep use of my mental willpower to overcome my aversion to lowering my arse into that chair. Or, I thought, the choice was to stand for an hour looking like a prat or at least a spare part. Even as I read the paper, my mind kept wandering back to what I was sitting in, and I wondered why the staff didn't have a bottle of that stain remover stuff to spray instantly on any spillage. I suppose when you're on minimum wage you really don't give a toss about what your customers have to sit in.

On boarding the train I see that, with her usual consideration for everyone's comfort, Maz has bought us seats near the toilets and the luggage racks. All it actually achieves is for John to hold up the progression of passengers on to the train.

'I must ensure our cases have the least possible chance of being damaged,' he advises us as he puts them first on the bottom rack, then stands back to consider, before deciding they would be better on the top rack. He glares at the first person to ask him to, 'hurry up mate.' I suppose that's what happens when you retire from work, you get used to taking your time over everything, and you would no longer consider that other people are in a hurry. He glares at Maz too, as though it is her

11

fault, and she decides that she and I will take the seats next to each other and leave him to sit alone facing us. There is definitely a hint of tension in the air.

I am wondering how they became good friends, as he's quite a lot of years older, retired and divorced. If I remember rightly, Maz told me once that they worked together when she was a secretary in the cop shop years ago. I remember her telling me she went straight from secretarial college, at the age of eighteen, into the 'lions den' of libidinous detectives. She worked in the typing pool with a group of older women in a very old building with cells in the basement. She said she could always tell when a meth's drinker had been in overnight, because the smell from the cells intermingled with the odour of the breakfasts being cooked for the policemen. She was soon nicknamed 'The Dolly Bird'. Even though women these days would object to a sexist remark like that, Maz told me it with pride. She said they learned how to handle things like 'sexual harassment', and in fact, it did not even cross their minds that that's what it was. She told me there were daily events of 'banter', which involved sexual innuendo, but it was accepted and not dwelt upon, as it is these days. It surprised me when she said that the women in the office had to share a toilet with male colleagues. I imagine John was one of the more painstaking of her colleagues, with emphasis on 'pain.'

As we approach Paris there is a feeling of excitement rising in my stomach that I have not experienced for a long time.

'Excusez-moi, Madame,' a dark-skinned man in blue overalls accidentally prods me in the back with his broom, as he sweeps the metro platform. Pretending not to notice that a frog has mistaken me for a woman, and hoping the others haven't noticed, I quickly leap on to the crowded metro train. As I stand there I start to muse on the word 'frog' in terms of French people. It goes against my viewpoint to call anyone from a

12

different culture by a derogatory name even if they supposedly got the term from eating frog's legs. I prefer to think that frog is made up of French (fr), origin (o), gentlemen (g). I know they call us Roast Beefs because we eat so much of the stuff but it doesn't bother me at all. Holding the pole in the metro carriage, my hand above Maz's, the sound of a man playing an accordion gives me imaginings of what it might be like in a French café. My tranquil thoughts are soon interrupted when we stop at the next station, and an array of people from all cultures force themselves in to the already limited space. We are crammed uncomfortably into the carriage as the train hurtles along, with me rebounding delightfully against Maz's chest like a kid on a bungee.

At the hotel, in Bagnolet, we have separate rooms and Maz and I have rooms opposite each other, with John's room further down the corridor. That first night, as we are all tired, we decide to stay at the hotel and pass an uneventful evening in the heavily carpeted hotel restaurant. There are a few businessmen in suits sitting alone at other tables and banal music is lilting softly in the background. We talk about the itinerary for the next few days, while we eat steak, which Maz advised me to order 'rare' the way the French like it.

'When in France, do as the French do,' she says. The blood runs out and soaks in to my 'frites', which makes them soggy, and barely edible, but I am determined to really live this French experience, and try not to think about Cruetz-feltz Jacob Disease.

To compliment the French culinary experience, we knock back two bottles of Claret between us, followed by a neat Cointreau.

'This is called a 'Digestif', Tony. It will help to settle your stomach after such a large meal. It contains carminative herbs which help to prevent flatulence,' John informs me as he raises his glass. We follow his lead, and clink our glasses together. John and Maz say 'bon santé' simultaneously. I can't resist adding a slightly mocking,

'Well John, here's to a wind-free night for you,' to which he narrows his eyes, adopting the appearance of someone who already has a pain in the gut.

Our rooms are on the top floor of the twelve-storey hotel, directly under the air conditioning units, which drone on and on, but after a while are strangely comforting, and you eventually become oblivious to any street noise.

To avoid having to pay for the expensive hotel continental breakfasts, Maz packed some breakfast cereal, plastic bowls, spoons and long-life milk. She knocks gently on my door in the morning. At the sound of her knock, I leap out of bed, spray some deodorant round the room, and open the door dressed only in my boxers. She hands me an already prepared bowl of cereal. I half expect her to sneak a quick look downwards, but she seems content to let her gaze drift round the room, and casually remarks on how untidy the room is after only one night. She appears to want to wait for me to finish the cereal, because she sits on the end of the bed and I munch merrily, looking forward to the day ahead.

'I'll wait for you to finish your cereal so that I can take the bowl to wash it up, and hide it back in the suitcase, then I've agreed we'll meet John down in the lobby in half an hour.' Through my munching, I nod and dribble milk down my chin, which in turn drips on to my bare stomach. 'I'll get my things together and meet you to take the lift down in say, twenty-five minutes,' she says, grabbing the empty bowl from me as she stands to leave.

There seems to be a delicious unsaid tension in the room. Ideas are leaping about in my head like it being only one step to falling down locked together on to the bed. Wanting to prolong that heady feeling, I have to think of something quickly, to keep her in the room a bit longer, so I ask her to comb my ponytail.

14

She smiles resignedly, takes my comb, and gently strokes. It is a pretty spine-tingling sensation, and she helpfully keeps the flat of her hand against the roots of my already thin hair, so that it is not being torn out, rendering me any balder.

We decide to pass most of the day at Pere Lachaise cemetery as it's near the hotel.

'This cemetery is over one hundred acres, and has a million graves, so I will purchase a map to use as a guide in order to locate the graves of interest,' John advises, before going to a little wooden hut to purchase the map he thinks he requires. Personally, I would rather just get on with walking the winding paths and come across the graves randomly. 'Now let's see, which grave interests you most Maz?' he asks, unfolding his new purchase, which starts flapping in the breeze. I am getting a bit frustrated with the delay, and he hasn't bothered asking which grave I would like to see, although to be fair, I don't actually know who is buried here. Maz says she wants to see the Jim Morrison grave, and I don't care I just want to get going. John locates it on the map, and we start walking along the narrow paths while she tells us about Jim Morrison. She seems to have read a lot about him and I can now guess why she has a giant black and white photo of him on the wall in her bathroom. She keeps us entertained by telling us about the old mystery of his death, and how people still make a vigil to his grave to light candles. She says he was a shy man, rather fancied himself more as a poet than singer, and kept his back to the audience when he sang in the early stages of his career. As he got in to drugs and drink he became an exhibitionist, and was arrested for opening the flies on his trousers and exposing himself.

'What a pity,' she sighs, and shakes her head. 'It is a real shame when talented, shy people get influenced like that. He was only twenty-seven when he died.'

'Was it a drugs overdose?' I enquire.

15

'Well, he was reportedly found in the bath but the mystery is, that no autopsy was ever carried out,' she replies, looking towards the sky as though to summon more memories. 'Do you know, before he came to Paris, Jim said to one of his musicians if it should it be reported that he died, he shouldn't believe it. He may have just decided to go missing, to go back to the happiness he had experienced before fame. He said that if he made contact by telephone, after the report of his death, his friend would know it was him, as he would say, "It's Mr Mojo Rising". It's in a biography by one his group members. When we go home I will give you the title. It is a sad story, all that talent wasted.'

'It makes you realise, doesn't it Maz, that the goal of attainment is not always the wisest path.'

'Yes, John, I agree. People are often so driven by attaining wealth that they forget the simple pleasures of life. I suppose he might have been happier writing his poetry, living a quieter life.'

We walk on to look at the grave of Colette, as Maz tells us the details of a book Colette wrote about the love affair between a very young man, and an older woman. Apparently Colette believed in sensuous pleasure as long as it did not give pain to others. All this talk of young man, older woman, and sensuous pleasure gives rise to not only, some might say, impious images but also to a pronounced bulge in my jeans. Maz however is oblivious, and talks like a lecturer merely trying to entertain us. She is never patronising, just likes to share her enthusiasm for subjects on which she has some knowledge. With another, deeper sigh, which sounds like longing, she moves us along and we pause briefly at the graves of Balzac, and then Oscar Wilde.

Back home, I have a book with a list of old Oscar Wilde's witticisms from which I often seek a good line to memorise, as you never know when you might need one. My favourite goes something like, '*I can resist everything, except temptation.*' I just wish I had some offer of temptation to try to resist.

Standing now, looking at the great man's burial place, and my dusty feet, I feel awe at the silence, the splendour, and the extravagance. Oddly, you would know you'd achieved the ultimate accolade if you end up buried here. I wonder if you know, before you die, that you deserve a space and whether you have to reserve?

We move on the metro to a place called Pigalle. Maz says she needs some plasters for her heels as her shoes have rubbed, and she is finding it painful to walk. We leave John waiting by the exit to Pigalle Metro so that he can peruse his street map, and we go across the road to a pharmacy. I am amazed at how dependent on drugs the Parisians must be, because there are the green flashing lights of pharmacies everywhere. I must be quickly adapting to French culture because, already, I find myself using the word 'pharmacy', when in England, I would say 'chemist'. As we enter, Maz has the opportunity to speak French properly for the first time. She orders, pays, takes the plasters and, as we leave, she puts her hand on my arm to stop me walking any further, 'Looks like John's having a conversation with a woman over there. Look.'

Sure enough, he is looking quite sheepish, staring at the ground, and then looking up at the woman with a weird contorted look. He seems to be half-smirking, and half frowning. They are definitely talking to each other, and we watch for a while. I am quite impressed that it hasn't taken him long to get stuck in. As we approach she looks agitated and rocks side to side before speaking to Maz,

'Pardon Madame, c'est votre mari, pardon, pardon,' and then she starts to rush away. Up close she is in her fifties, dirty-looking, wearing a grey dress, and her face has several boils with little yellow peaks.

'Can't leave you alone for a minute can we mate?' I joke with John. He is ashen, and angry,

'That was a bloody Tom, I've just been propositioned, and I couldn't make her go away. I kept saying, "je ne comprend

17

pas", but she was determined. I've only been in Paris less than a day, I am left alone on this corner for five minutes, and an old Tom wants to do a deal with me. It's disgusting.' He is brushing at the arms of his rather expensive-looking jacket as though she has deposited some sort of debris on it.

'That must have been some ordeal,' I say, trying to hold in my laughter.

'There is rudeness and lewdness everywhere you go nowadays,' he retorts looking directly at me.

Later in the afternoon, en route by foot to the Eiffel Tower, I really see Paris through the screen of my digital camera. I take picture after picture like an obsessive, ducking, squatting, stretching trying to get the best shots ready for Facebook. The old guy starts to get annoyed.

'Yes, Tony, you have taken that picture before, about twenty times in fact.' He stands with his hands behind his back, in the policeman's pose he should have ditched ten years ago. 'We've got to get a move on, the rendezvous is in vingt minutes au Eiffel Tower.' Man, his attempt at French is pathetic. He's got his map and magnifying glass out. Why can't he just go with the flow?

One excellent thing just happened. We stood on a street corner, with no sign of the Eiffel Tower, and then Maz starts pointing beyond the wall.

'Look round the side of this building Tony,' she says, and there it is. It is massive, and has literally blown me away. Waiting for us, underneath the foot of the tower, are Philippe, Xavier, Jacques and Soumaya.

'Heh, me old buddies,' I call out, while running to them, unable to stop the beam that has swallowed up my face, and then they all in turn engulf me with kisses. In England, no bloke would get near to planting one on me.

Philippe was the one that I knew first, a bit of a rebel. He enjoyed playing his guitar, and he could play us music on Maz's keyboard, stuff he had just heard on the radio or on the stereo, right out of his head. One night he took his guitar and sang her a Bob Dylan song that he learnt in order just to please her. He told her that too, you know, that he'd learnt it just to please her, and said it with a smile on his face. You could see that she was well-over the moon. He liked the daughter well and truly, which is probably why he came back to stay every summer. Then one year, when we were all about eighteen, and they were twenty-one, he brought Xavier after they both graduated from the Sorbonne. Maz let Xavier sleep in the loft room of her house, and he ended up living there for a year. That was a bit of a weird time. While the rest of us were still chancing our luck with her daughter, (even though by then she had a boyfriend), Maz was doing translations, and listening to Dylan, with Xavier. He didn't bother with the rest of us, just took her over, creeping in like a shady invader.

Jacques, who is Philippe's younger brother, spent some holidays in Maz's house about two years later. He's a lanky actor now, and has one hell of an impressive moustache. Philippe, with dreadlocks longer than my ponytail, and a wide-mouth smile, looks like a white Bob Marley having a marvellous day. One summer, I remember Philippe said he was fed up with being a lad, and seeing so many girls, so he had made a decision that he was going to marry the next girl he met. Whoa, I thought, that's dangerous, the next girl you meet and you're just off to the Moroccan desert. True to his word, he meets gorgeous little Soumaya. To please her old man, in order that he could marry her, and bring her back to Paris, he changed his name to Ishmael. I really admired his dedication.

'We shan't be going up the tower today Tony, as I am prone to a little vertigo,' advises the jolly copper.

'Je propose un restaurant pres de mon apartement,' says Philippe smiling, and indicating for us to follow him. We start mooching after him.

I can't believe how much dog shit I have to avoid, and wonder if that's why there are streams of water running down the roads by the kerbs, so people can kick the shit into it. By the amount of brown footprints on the pavement, it looks like quite a few got unlucky.

'We are going to show you the Arc de Triomphe before going to the restaurant. You might want to save your camera battery until we reach the Arc.' John hisses the words at me between his teeth, like a threat, while he points at his city guide. He probably thinks he's succeeded in making me feel like the larvae of an insect he'd prefer didn't hatch.

We arrive at this amazing architectural building, and sitting on a cold stone platform, I am thinking about the soldiers who died in World War One and the Unknown Soldier being buried beneath us, when Maz takes her shoes off saying her feet hurt. Before you can say 'leaping frog', Xavier is kneeling in front of her, looking like he is a connoisseur of feet or something. Then, he takes each foot in turn, and massages them for her. The cunning bastard.

It's a sunny February day, and several armed gendarmes on roller skates skim by. It's bizarre how the hazy smog blurs their outlines as they skate on down the Champs Elysees like they're fuzzy, the fuzzy 'Fuzz', that idea amuses me and I chuckle to myself. Jacques explains the presence of the police, by telling us that Paris is hosting the final of the Six Nations Rugby this evening between England and France.

Every time we pass an armed gendarme, Maz stares guiltily at my rucksack like I've got dope the size of a rugby ball in it, so I loosen the strap and keep swinging it over my shoulder. Actually, I smoked the small amount I had last night while I stood at my window watching the hooker framed in another window across the street. It was a red light in the window, on the first floor of a block opposite, which first caught my eye. Then I noticed the hooker. She was sitting sideways on a table near the window ledge, wearing a black basque. It was great watching from above so she couldn't see me. To attract the attention of men walking by, she raised her leg, the one nearest the window, so they would have full view of her stockings. She looked bloody uncomfortable, perched like a blubbery seal on the edge of a rock. This image, I thought, did everything to dispel the myth I'd heard about all French women being thin. Yet, on thinking about it, she may not have been French. I didn't see anyone sneak in to the building, but several men stopped to have a gander. I hoped she might forget to close her curtains if a punter finally took her up, but I got bored waiting. Maz looks happier than I've seen her in a while. It suits her to be in this cultural capital. I can now say Philippe is as sneaky as Xavier because he just darted over to a market shoe stall, and bought Maz a pair of comfortable slip-on black shoes. I'll take her to a Jazz Café later tonight if I can dump John.

The restaurant, Philippe has brought us to, 'Les Artistes', is small like someone's front room. I get to sit opposite John and a massive mirror, so I am in the unfortunate position of not only having to face the Smiling Assassin, but also of having to look at the back of his balding silver head. Call me sensitive, or perhaps perceptive, but I have this stomach-churning feeling that something dire is about to happen. Maybe what's set off my nausea is Xavier's food choice. He ordered some lightly fried testicles and is about to tuck into them.

The Franglais is good, and after a few glasses of wine we all seem to be experts at speaking each other's language and I am beginning to settle. Soumaya accuses Philippe of fancying the waitress so Maz tells him to say, 'I love you Soumaya' every day, then she won't feel jealous. We're all quite drunk and full of French cuisine. As we leave the restaurant to go on to Philippe's flat, Jacques dramatically sweeps out his arm and offers it to Maz. The creep.

21

CHAPTER THREE

Shoving and laughing, the seven of us enter the small lift on the ground floor of the apartment block where Philippe and Soumaya live. Xavier pushes the button for the eleventh floor. I am looking forward to getting up to their flat because Maz told me the last time she visited, Soumaya taught her how to belly-dance and they put on a show for Philippe. I wouldn't mind seeing a bit of that.

The lift starts then, after rapidly ascending some distance, stops abruptly. With no hesitation, as though this is a regular occurrence in Paris, Xavier presses the emergency button and a French woman's voice immediately responds. Xavier translates and tells us an engineer has been called. It's soon hard to breathe in this tiny enclosed space. The grey alloy walls surrounding us suddenly become noticeable, menacing, and it feels like we are in a metal tomb. Hoping no-one notices the rising panic I am feeling, I surreptitiously start looking round for an air vent. There does not appear anything that remotely looks like it could supply air but the speaker system, which I hope doubles as an air supply. It becomes so hot that we dump our coats on the floor not wanting to hold them close to our bodies.

'Are we supposed to get close to the floor to conserve air?' Maz says, panicking, and I am so stuffed with Comfit du Canard I feel I might puke.

'That's a bit of an absurd idea when you consider the size of our arses,' I respond.

'Why don't you bloody well shut up Tony, you've been getting on my nerves since we got here,' John says, turning towards the steel doors which he begins to prise open with his fingers. He and Xavier manage to force a gap of half an inch, which lets in a little air but they have to keep letting go and the doors close tight again. Soumaya presses the emergency bell, shouting slightly hysterically in French that 'maman', referring to Maz, is distressed.

'I really need a wee,' Maz whispers, looking at the three square inches of floor space that remain visible.

'We have one empty coke bottle between us,' I say, pulling one out of my rucksack like a magician and giving a big smile to reassure her. Although this is a genuine offer of help she disappointingly doesn't take the bottle.

The engineer arrives, but is not competent enough to do anything more than push a screwdriver between the doors for our entire oxygen supply. We have been shut in for two hours. Sweat is pronounced on everyone's brow and mine is worse than anyone's, it is dripping. We are advised that a specialist engineer has been called. I am very sceptical about the word 'specialist' in relation to this apartment block.

The atmosphere is a bit panic-making and I can feel, and hear, my stomach juices squirting through my colon. Man, I have never been so aware of them. Xavier faces the door, bolt upright, like he's a soldier or something. John grinds his teeth through a grimace, and Jacques has his hand on Maz's shoulder as though to keep her calm. Philippe holds tightly to Soumaya, who soon sinks to the floor as a stink, as rancid as a cowshed, fills the space. Great, now we have a dose of methane boosting our limited air supply.

In our lethargic state, no-one owns up to letting one go, or even acknowledging that they can smell anything. After a further hour, in which we are much too hot and scared to speak, without warning, the doors open. It is apparent that the lift is stuck between two floors and everyone wants to try to squeeze out. But ever-cautious John says that if the lift starts to move we could lose a body part. Lucky he said that, because there is a forceful jolt and it starts being winched downwards in very slow hefty jerks until, after some considerable time, we hit the ground hard, and are plunged into complete darkness. It is also fucking freezing. Man, we can't even see each other. The woman's voice pierces the darkness to advise us that we are in the sub-basement, which I must say does not come as much surprise. Xavier translates as she goes on to tell us that she is in the process of trying to contact the janitor. It transpires that the janitor, who has the only key to the sub-basement, is at the final of the rugby between France and England in Stade de France.

The need to pee is getting the better of me too. Even though I'm no prude I don't want to embarrass myself by pissing in to a plastic bottle, and besides it is pitch black so my aim might not be too good. I am even hoping that nothing happens to the chubby copper while we are at the mercy of incompetents. Although we can't see each other, there is the impression of solidarity between us, which I can sense in the air. If we get out of this, we'll all have something in common to harp on about in years to come. Eventually, after shivering uncontrollably for what feels like about an hour, in the black, frightening coldness, voices penetrate, and a light startles us. I look at my watch and see that it is twelve minutes past midnight, so the jazz club idea is already scuppered. The shuffling janitor, who must have stayed to watch the end of the match, says in a miserable tone of voice, that England beat France, so at least that's a bit of good news.

'We should be very wary of making it known that we are English on our way back to the hotel, in case of trouble,' says Jolly John.

'I am sure we can manage to convince people that we are French John, especially with your command of the language and my five words of French vocabulary,' I respond, letting out my pent-up irritation.Philippe asks if everyone would like to come up to his apartment for coffee and there is an instant collective reply of, 'Non.'

The next day, when Maz brings me my breakfast, she says that John is ill in bed with, what he thinks, is a urine infection from having to 'retain his water' for so long in the lift. She doesn't wait for me to eat my cereal today, just says she will see me a little later. I hope therefore to have her to myself for the day. Just to be sure John is kept entertained in his bedroom, and does not change his mind about coming out, I rush straight out to buy him a book, from the bookseller just along the street from the hotel. And, barely able to contain my glee, at my amazing good luck, at finding an English novel, I take it to him.

I knock at his door and after a few minutes he slowly opens the door still dressed in his long grey striped pyjama bottoms and looking haggard.

'Here, I got you this book old chap. Don't try to come out too soon,' I say in my most sympathetic voice. He looks vaguely surprised at my generosity as he removes the book slowly from the white paper bag. When he has extracted it, his glare of contempt makes me smile with pleasure - my choice is outstanding.

I knock on Maz's door and tell her I bought John an English book.

'You found him an English book, that's kind of you. What's the title?' she asks.

'*Merde Happens*,' I say with a happy grin.

CHAPTER FOUR

It seems pretty obvious to me that Maz has other things on her mind rather than coming out to enjoy the day with me. I can see this head of hair in the bed as I glance over her shoulder while we speak at the door of her room. The nameless head is keeping his face well-hidden, and probably doesn't realise I can see the hair. The black hair poking above the sheets gives me the impression that one of the others got lucky. I can't believe she would let someone randomly stay the night with her, she is not that type of woman, or at least I suspect that she isn't. It has to be someone she knows well. I feel like I want to plead with her to come out in to the city. She realises what I can see beyond her, in her bed.

'Get yourself off to an exhibition and I'll see you later. Oh, and that is not what it seems,' she indicates towards the bed. 'He just needed somewhere to stay and I slept on the pull-out bed,' she says dismissing me with a flick of her hand, and I feel the money spent on a book for John is wasted. I mooch off to the hotel lobby and pick up a leaflet about the Louvre, smiling at the uninterested and uninteresting male receptionist. No matter what time we have been in or out of the hotel he is always sitting there looking like a stuffed penguin with a snooty sneer on his face.

I queue along with about a thousand others to get in to The Louvre, and have time to take in its mind-blowing size. It amazes me that a king thought he was important enough to have it built for him. It says, in my information leaflet, that during

26

the French Revolution it was turned into a museum. My principles regarding Royalty, mean that I am very happy to know the building went out of the hands of the Royals and into the public domain. I do not believe in all that Royalty stuff and I am glad therefore, that I haven't been put off a gander round the place. You wouldn't get me looking round old Buck Palace. Anyway I have a plan. I am going to see some of the paintings and archaeology then I am going to hang around the Mona Lisa. Because everyone wants to see that picture, I am thinking that there might be a chance to speak with a girl. I imagine, and hope, she will be a slim young thing with a hint of a tan and a mind to match mine, perhaps English-speaking French with long shimmering dark hair. I'll ask her to take a coffee with me and she will speak with a delicious French lilt.

After taking some photos of the glass pyramid, at last I'm in the Great Hall. Just the size of the hall makes me feel overwhelmed and a bit tired, so I abandon my plan to look at the archaeology and paintings and revert to the second stage of my plan. I position myself by the Mona Lisa. What a disappointment that painting is, yeah okay her eyes follow you round because I move in every direction to check it out, but the picture is so small. My feet start feeling like they are made of elastic bands that are snapping in my shoes, so I bang the toes on the floor to relieve the pain, while emitting the odd 'ah, ah,' as the stinging sensation shoots up my legs. I sense that these odd movements, with me jumping up and down like a meerkat, are probably doing nothing for my potential pulling power.

'Jeez, look at her eyes Connie, they follow you all around.'

'Heh, Harrison look at her eyes, does she remind you of me?' It's a haggard-looking woman with a loud, annoying American accent standing next to the picture placing her face as close to the glass surround as it allows, wanting her husband to endorse her beauty, the poor bloke. 'Yeah, honey you've still got it,' he replies as automatically as he has been primed to do.

27

In the half an hour that I have been here I've heard the same kind of inane comments. It reminds me of a song about obese women who can no longer see their knees, and all the old unattractive people with wobbly bits who go to see the Mona Lisa. I understand the meaning of that song now, having stood here long enough. The songwriter must have stood right where I'm standing, then gone back to America and written, probably one of the most dramatic songs of all time, about pretence. I hate that sham stuff, people visiting museums and putting on pretence of knowing about art when there is not a brain cell between them. One thing is for sure, I want to buy more books, keep up with my high quality reading, get a '*Kindle*' and continue improving my brain. I want to meet a girl with the same ideals. Shallowness pisses me off.

I get out of the Louvre and meander down the Rue de Rivoli before jumping on to a metro train back to the hotel. Old Xavier happens to be in the lobby, which occurs to me is highly suspicious as he has black hair.

'Alright mate, how ya doing?'

'Ah, bien, bien, et toi? I 'ave spoken avec Jacques, 'e says 'e will take you to a Jazz club tonight avec Maz.' Then I remember that Jacques has black hair, and so do most of the damn waiters. I feel a little paranoid.

'I'll give it a miss tonight mate, have a quiet night in. See you in England when you next visit. Remember, keep on trucking and don't let the bastards grind you down.'

'Et toi aussi, Tony, et toi aussi.' He gives me a grateful smile and heads quickly towards the revolving doors. He is about three years older than me, and I think he's a smart guy, one of those intellectuals who don't ram opinions at you. Although he took all Maz's attention when he stayed in her house for a year, he was able to talk about any book, film or music. Incredibly, he seemed to know so much about any topic that his conversation was never limited. He never drank alcohol, didn't smoke, had some weird tastes in food, but he

28

was quiet and never offensive to anyone. I suppose he gets time for all the reading and film-watching because he's stayed single. Although I'd like a girlfriend, and most of my thoughts are dominated by how to get one, that kind of intellectual single life appeals to me too. Part of me wants to run after him, to ask him if he stayed last night but I decide to leave it. Maz will tell me if she decides to. I feel jangled and my head is full of ideas about the direction I want my life to go. It's annoyingly never static, as I haven't yet fully formed my game plan.

Before Paris I had it in my head that I would meet a girl, get laid, live together, visit a few places and it didn't extend beyond that. Now ideas are jumping and, the thought I had in the Louvre, regarding reading more, is developing into the vision of me in a flat, my books on shelves around the room. I think I would like to meet an intellectual woman, and while we would be having great discussions I would smoke a pipe. Then I imagine I would enjoy taking her for meals and visits. We would share these passions, have mind-blowing sex, and I might even take up writing. May be I'm turning in to a nerd.

Now that I think the 'suspect' has left her room, I knock on Maz's door and she opens it to let me in. She is dressed in jeans, tee shirt and her new flat black shoes.

'Well Tony, how about a walk in the Tuilleries?'

'Bien sur, Madame,' I say to impress her

'I'll just check on John, make sure he's got drink and food, then we'll be on our way. Make sure you feel comfortably dressed, because it will be quite a walk along the banks of the Seine.'

I am awe-struck by the amount of book-sellers and artists at their own stalls along the whole route. Maz has to keep moving me along, as I want to look at everything. This is not your tacky souvenir type-stuff, it is real art by real artists. We make our way into the Tuilleries gardens and Maz takes my arm.

'Isn't it wonderful Tony? Look at the fountains, and I like

the feeling of walking on sand, it makes you feel light somehow.'

I agree with her I, too, feel happy and light-hearted especially seeing the Louvre in the distance and thousands of people strolling together in the February sunshine. I have a great feeling of peace, and the feel of her arm in mine is rousing. A scruffy old woman wearing a thick headscarf interrupts our peaceful strolling. She squats to the floor and picks up a wide gold ring. She places it in the palm of her extended hand, shows it to us, and then presses it into my hand. I take it to one side and look it over, noting the hallmark and weight. She indicates to me, and says in broken English, 'For you, no fit me.' Delighted, I hang on to it and we begin to walk away.

'Money, money...' she follows us holding out her hand, 'money for food.' I get out my wallet and hand her fifteen euros. We start to walk away.

'More money, more money,' she tugs at my arm.

'No!' shouts Maz, as she grabs the ring from me and hands it back to the woman, who quickly scuttles away. Maz takes my hand and drags me up some steps to a place called L'Orangery. She tells the security guard that we have just lost fifteen euros to a woman who was pretending to find gold rings on the ground. Another Englishman appears from inside the building and says he fell for the same scam and lost one hundred euros. I am standing utterly silent and bemused. From my understanding of the odd word, here and there, I find I am able to interpret what Maz is saying to the security man. She points out the woman, and tells the security man to go and arrest her as she is in the process of carrying out the scam again, with, what Maz thinks, must be fake gold rings. He shrugs at her and merely says, 'Les Roma's, bad, bad.' I am a bit pissed off with Maz for handing back the ring, even if it wasn't real gold, because at least I would have had something to show for my money and, worse, she doesn't seem in any mood to continue holding my arm.

'Learn from that, Tony, bargains nearly always come with a catch.'

Later we take a break, enjoy a baguette and bottle of good wine together, followed by a very late afternoon trip to Montmartre and the Artists Quarter where famous artists like Toulouse-Lautrec lived and worked. I look up at the little turret rooms above us, and imagine what it must have been like to live in such an environment. They surely always had other like-minded people around with whom to share a coffee or alcohol, and to be able to talk about their work in progress. I like that idea, to meander out of your apartment at any time of day, and meet up with other intellectuals in the cafes, or to be able to sit and ponder about your unfinished work. I suppose I would probably do a lot more pondering than work, if I'm honest.

To finish our trip, in the early evening, as it is beginning to get dark, Maz takes me to see the outside of The Moulin Rouge, which is quite spectacular, as it is all lit up. She tells me about the dancing girls, and how many of the impressionist artists in the nineteenth century used them as models, or indeed for sexual favours. There was one, she says, called 'La Goulue' who could turn her leg and high kick so that she could flip men's hats off whilst showing off the heart embroidered on her knickers.

We take a gander round the Museum of Erotic Art, looking at all the ancient, and modern, methods man has used to portray eroticism, which I am enjoying and finding intensely interesting. When we reach the fourth floor, which has no windows, and must once have been an attic, I become aware of a man, who at first I thought was a statue, as he starts to move. He is dressed in silver Lurex Speedo-type underpants, and his face and body are painted in a sort of glossy silver. His eyes deliberately engage ours, then he moves his arms like a graceful ballerina and tries his best to tantalise us with slow, beckoning, seductive movements like a kind of erotic dance.

31

Unfortunately, a thick smell of stale sweat wafts up and impales itself in my nostrils. Any erotic stimulation I had been experiencing, by looking at the art, is evaporated by me wondering whether the geezer is still wearing the same Lurex that he started the week in. By the stench he is giving off, it could have been a month.

It is the last night at the hotel and Maz just wants to go back to pack and relax, so I am alone in my room and pretty bored. Without my usual stimulant to occupy me, after a shower, I lie naked on my bed and think of Maz. I let my fantasies run wild. I imagine taking a bottle of wine to her room where she has stepped out of a hot bath and she answers my knock wearing nothing but a silken gown, her nipples protruding through the flimsy material. She invites me in, and I visualize us sitting on the bed, our backs against propped-up pillows. We drink, we talk and the tension builds as I imagine sitting as close as I dare, our thighs rubbing. In my wild imaginings she says I can take a shower. I picture myself showering hastily, and returning from the bathroom with a towel wrapped round my waist, using the excuse that I don't like putting dirty clothes back on and she is tipsy, and laughing, as I bound on to the bed, losing the towel in the process. My imagination is hot now, especially about bounding on to the bed and her seeing my large pulsing dick. Her eyes widen, as does the gown, exposing her nakedness. My fantasist-self leans in and strokes her stomach. In the next instant she is writhing on top of me, groaning, urging, sliding her clit along the length of my shaft, bringing herself to the point of orgasm. I am imagining rubbing her nipples, and then her telling me to suck them. I roll her over and she is telling me I am the hardest, most exciting man she has ever had, as I prepare to stick my cock that's like a hot throbbing.........

'Tony, Tony, open the door I need some bottled water.' It's that pissing copper, knocking on my door with timing almost as immaculate as his trouser creases.

32

'Give me a minute old chap,' I shout back, as I wait for my old chap to diminish enough to pull on my boxers and I trip, gasping, towards the door.

'Come on! Open the door. What the hell is keeping you? I can't stand out in the corridor like this.'

'I said, I won't be a minute,' I pant in exasperation, as I yank the door open.

'Can you nip down to the bar and get me some bottled water I can't drink the stuff from the tap. One has to be careful, especially in a big city in a foreign country. I must have bottled. Clearly I can't ask a woman to go to the bar, it's not manly.'

'Don't worry, I'll get dressed myself and go down and get it for you,' I notice I am still a little breathless, but pleased that I have not given in to showing any further annoyance.

'Even though you didn't call in to see if I am improved,' he chastises me, 'I feel much better and will be ready for our trip home tomorrow although, as you probably understand, I don't feel well enough to change out of pyjamas to go all the way down to the bar,' he says indicating to his pyjama bottoms and bare feet, which I am sure is to try to provoke my sympathy. 'I hope you have spent the evening in suitable preparation for tomorrow, Tony.'

'Yes John, I have been fully engaged in packing my three pairs of shreddies, two tee shirts and pair of jeans,' I reply, but immediately regret my slip in to a contemptuous response, so decide to humour him. 'I will go and get your water, still or sparkling?'

'Still please.'

After I've taken him the water, I actually do pack my rucksack and spend some time considering how I can make myself appear more mature. It becomes apparent, after a lot of looking in the mirror, that I might, unfortunately, have to lose the ponytail.

CHAPTER FIVE

About an hour ago I uploaded my photos on to Facebook so my hundred or so friends can see what I experienced in Paris. Me at L'Arc de Triomphe, me at Tour Eiffel, me at the bridge with padlocks, and I deliberately missed out mentioning the bit about the lift. I give old Jolly John his due, three hundred photos does seem a bit over the top now. Anyway, something good's come of my upload because one of my old mates, Cheddar, just contacted me with an instant message asking me to go speed-dating with him this evening. It's only a tenner and I haven't seen him for two years.

Well, as I said, tonight is the night and I am experiencing slightly elevated feelings. I remember my mum listening to a song about tonight being the night, and I liked the imagery in it, which had something about removing a pretty French gown and all that. She used to put the LP on the record player, scratch the needle across the record until she found the start of that song and dance round the living room. I used to wonder if she was trying to imagine a life where someone would take that much interest in her. It didn't happen for her as far as I can tell. Anyway the image of her podgy little figure having a French gown slipping from her shoulders is unbearably grim.

In preparation for tonight's soiree at the speed-dating thing I go to the hairdresser and pluck up the courage to have my ponytail cut off. I have the full works of wash, cut and blowdry. Marius the mincer is doing the work for me. God, that man can mince. He would be six inches shorter if he took off his platform shoes, which are white with little splashes of diamonds over the toes, and I think I will actually go blind if the light catches his shiny shirt in the mirror. I have never seen a bloke with such a thin waist. At least he is wearing a wide-buckled belt, which thankfully keeps his trousers from sliding down over his hips sparing me having to see three-quarters of his designer underpants. I think I'm pretty trendy but these blokes who walk about with that much of their pants showing make me feel sick, I think I might end up seeing a skid mark and then wonder if they sat somewhere like the bus seat before me. I am actually quite pleased with my short hair and feel it makes me look more macho.

When I return home, I take a hot shower and as I start to dress, I catch a glimpse of my face, which has turned a rather strawberry shade of red, because I let the water beat down on it, thinking it might tighten the muscles and straighten out the couple of wrinkles by my eyes. A stone hits my window, so I lean out and Cheddar is grinning up at me,

'Come on tosser, get your arse into gear or we'll be late.' He's wearing a suit, Mr immaculate, all tanned, toothy, and confident-looking, waiting for me with one hand casually tucked in his trouser pocket. I assume he used the other hand to toss the stone at my window. We nicknamed him 'Cheddar' when we were young teenagers on account of his feet. At bedtime, his mum used to go in to his room, pick up the socks he had discarded from that day, and throw them out of the window. She told us she would invariable pick them up the next morning when it was safe to do so.

In preparation for tonight, I spent some time choosing light blue jeans and a white tee shirt with the slogan '*0-60 in Sixty Seconds, I Come Quickly!*' as I thought the girls would remember that when they fill in the form to say who they'd like to see again.

'Okay matey, right with you,' I shout down to him. I grab my keys and wallet and hack down the stairs of my sister's house. She owns it, I pay rent for a room but I can use all the facilities. It beats living with mum, and I could bring a girl back if I could get one.

We hand our tenners to a bouncer in a dickie bow tie who checks us in against the details Cheddar emailed in advance. We then go through to a hall, which is actually the gym of a college, and has the left over distinct aroma of sweaty feet. Someone hands me a glass of white wine and I down it. As I glance round the room, I quickly calculate that it is not a well-organised event because everyone is of varying age. There must be fifty of us losers here with the purpose of finding a partner. The intrigue is in wondering who I'll score a hit with. Cheddar says he's got a girl a few times using this method, and it's a 'cinch.'

'Just tell her she's beautiful, you tosspot, it gets them every time. Don't waste time asking what her hobbies are, you can find that out when she hooks on the line and you get to see her again,' he advises. I start acting like one of those annoying nodding toy dogs you see in car windows, it's making my neck ache and I feel like I've developed lockjaw with all the smiling.

The women are asked to sit behind desks and note pads are placed in front of them. We blokes are given a number to stick on our tops. I am number five and as I pin it to my tee shirt I make sure my slogan is still visible. A bloke in sandals with a heavy black beard, who looks like he could be the leader of a cult, instructs us that we have four minutes with each female, and when a whistle blows we have to move on to the next woman. There seem to be more women than men. Bloody hell, what if all the younger ones choose me? I'm a made man.

The first on my list is Madge, and before I find her desk, I get a horny image in my head of Madonna wearing black stockings. I am soon disappointed to discover that this Madge is a skinny girl of about twenty-five with bad skin and a hair bun. Although I feel a moment of empathy with her in having parents like mine who gave her a name open to ridicule, I don't want to impress her too much so I say,

'This is the best of all possible worlds,' and give her a weird smile like I'm two pence short of a pound.

'Oh, you like Voltaire, I like the way he satirizes the human condition,' she replies making a mark on her writing pad. This is horrible, I actually enjoy philosophy but I do not like the appearance of her so I look towards my next encounter and hope my wandering eye puts her off.

About forty minutes into the event I meet a girl who at last sparks my mild interest. Blonde, low-cut tee shirt, a ring on each finger, loads of red lipstick. Look I am not here to meet the girl of my dreams but this will do for a date.

'You're beautiful,' I say confidently.

'Thanks mate, you're the tenth who's said that. Haven't you got something more interesting to say? And, if your tee shirt is correct, all I can say is give me Eric Clapton any day.'

'Old "slow-hand" you mean?' I say, feeling rather pleased with myself that I am quick witted enough to pick up on her insinuation. I am about to tell her I imagine I can do a good job with a slow hand, but decide to say nothing. Instead, I give her my version of a seductive, knowing smile.

'Yeah, so why are you boasting you come quickly? That's better for girls to do isn't it, when we don't keep you waiting too long and you don't have to work too hard?' Now I am wondering if she's being deliberately provocative and I get all confused, feeling like a prat. Anyway, after a few further exchanges I decide I don't like the way she speaks, it's weird, like she copied her accent off a television programme. As the whistle blows, she leans across the desk giving me a view of herchest, and strokes the length of my middle finger seductively with one finger,

'That's what I'll want from you,' she says, then laughs hard, and although I already know it from my list, she says her name is Bee, 'As in buzzin' just so's you'll remember if you gets put on me list.'

I move on. It's hot, and the noise is hell in the hall. I can hear laughter and shrieks above the constant droning undertone of voices and my ears are buzzing. I calculate I must have another twenty women to interview and be interviewed by. I take another glass of wine and sit on a black plastic chair facing my next interviewee, Beverley. Beverley tells me proudly that she is sixty-four. At the beginning of the evening I was trying to remember little things about each woman but I don't want to commit to memory being chatted up by a woman of sixty-four.

The whistle sounds, and it's on to Dexi, in her fifties, likes to 'swing' she says. I really imagine her on a garden swing until she asks if I like a bit of bondage, and how do I feel about being tickled with a feather while being strapped to a bedpost as others look on. She says she wants a guy to go with her to the next party, and asks if I would 'rise to the occasion'. The confidence of some people amazes me, or perhaps they just don't give up hope? This one really is confident, despite having hair worn away on the crown, perhaps from all that writhing on a bed, badly stained teeth and no shape. I know that, about her shape, because she stands to show me her micro-mini skirt. I can only suppose she is hoping it will turn me on. As she spins round, she drops her pen, which I suspect is on purpose, bends over to pick it up, and I nearly faint at the vile sight of her flabby little buttocks parted by a leopard-skin thong. From this experience I have learnt that thin women can have buttocks as badly wrinkled as a heavy smoker's face. At this moment, I decide I want a smoke more than a woman. I am intrigued though as to whether any of the women have been impressed enough by me to put me as a favourite. I have to wait a week to find out.

CHAPTER SIX

You may be wondering why I don't particularly talk about my work. But, perhaps you would like a bit of background so to speak. I try to live an exciting and varied life outside of work. Work is something I have to do to get some dosh but this particular job is not something I'd choose to do. The building, where I work, is one of those built to 'enhance the landscape' of the town, or so the planners say. It is tall, and can be seen from any vantage point. It has a bloody great spire on top of it. It's weird that churches are no longer built with spires but the planners put them on offices instead. Office policies seem like a new form of religion, with all the control and political correctness.

So, I work for a large accountancy firm in the Human Resources Department keeping the files in order. The windows are all tinted blue so we can't see what kind of weather we're missing or be tempted to look out and daydream.

'Get an email sent round to everyone Tony, telling them there will be a meeting at three this afternoon in number three boardroom, then organise the coffee, tea and I think we will offer Viennese Whirls.' That's Georgina my immediate boss. She is a control freak, head of HR and full of 'team bonding' ideas. She is immaculate and I hate her. 'Hate' is not a word that is allowed in this company. She has ruled out gossip, antipathy, sadness, anger and any other emotion you can think of. All the accountants go around with a perpetual false smile and bonhomie.

I notice that everyone is becoming identical with no personality. The women are beginning to look alike with their botox injections, lip fillers, whitened teeth set against fake tans, fake French nail varnish, and similar hairstyles. It's a weird environment for me to work in but I have managed to keep the job for ten years and, believe me, I really am only in it for the money. I use the place for my own ends, and generally try to keep home as a place of sanctuary. While I'm at work I do my emails to mates, read the newspaper online and there's also something quite satisfying about trying to keep my bowel movements for work time so I get paid for having a dump.

We have to all wear suits and one of the company rules for men is short hair, but when I sported a ponytail they did make an exception for it, as I don't go out to meet the clients, and generally remain unseen by the public. Or, perhaps the chairman fancied me when I had my interview. Now my ponytail has gone I feel freakishly like all the other short-haired arseholes. I won't socialise with them, apart from when it is required for 'team building' because I would be afraid of succumbing to gossip and what I say being reported back. You really have to watch your back, there is always someone ready to dob you in to the bosses. These days you never know when an employee has switched on a mobile phone to record a crucial comment and then you'd be in the crap house.

The chairman is an okay kind of guy with a genuine smile, and he only comes in to the office about four times a year. You should see Georgina get in a panic when he's coming in. She brings in a can of that spray polish stuff and starts polishing everything in sight even though there are a firm of cleaners who come in to the offices every evening. She puts a bottle of best brandy and glasses on his desk, alongside a large white jotter housed in a leather-bound surround. Each time he comes in, he brings her a big bunch of lilies, which quickly start to give me watering eyes, dripping nose and a feeling like I've got both asthma and hayfever. It says on the wrapping that they are guaranteed to last two weeks but, believe me, they have the capacity to last three. After the first time, of suffering their effects for three weeks, I learnt to offer to put them in the vase for her. I add a little water and top it up with coffee so they quickly start to dehydrate, then they wilt and the petals turn brown. Georgina gets rid of them when they are brown-tinged because they no longer 'aesthetically enhance the office.'

'What's on the agenda for this meeting then Georgina?'

'I am thinking of putting motivational posters along the corridors for esteem-building purposes and I would like everyone to input their ideas. Things that will grow their confidence, something like, "We are the Chosen Ones, An Accountant's Life is a Happy One" you know, that kind of thing. Plus, we should discuss the next bonding session'. For some reason the word 'bonding' makes awful apparitions of Dexi from the Speed Dating experience enter my head and I feel a bit unwell.

'I'll get the email sent, and set up the room for the meeting right away,' I say in agreement, heading towards the door. Even though I feel nauseous, I manage to turn and flash the required smile. I dread the team building weekends, everyone is so scared of letting a bit of personality escape but sometimes you get to see an inkling of what a person could have been, or is, outside of the political correctness imposed by the Company.

Strolling in to town on my lunchbreak, I feel the need to visit the gents in the big shopping mall. This is not usual because, as I said before, I usually store my toilet needs for work time. There is a glossy advert pinned to the toilet wall by the door about tooth whitening. It catches my eye because the images are of geezers with girls draped all over them. They all have sparkling white teeth. As I am on a mission to improve my image, I ring there and then and book an appointment for this evening. Perhaps I'm on the slippery slope to fakery.

CHAPTER SEVEN

I venture into this real girlish-looking beauty salon, and a fit girl in a black tight-fitting uniform looks up my booking on a computer screen. I am feeling annoyed for succumbing to advertising propaganda. She asks me to take a seat next to a coffee table piled with celebrity magazines, and I pick one up to flick through. It is full of photos of celebrities with fake smiles showing glowing white teeth. It pisses me off that in every one of those photos the gormless grin seems to be saying nothing else about the subject except, 'look at my teeth, how great do I look? ' That's what comes over to me. Photographers seem to have lost the ability to capture the real essence of their subjects, which means they all look like they lack any kind of personality. I like seeing the old black and white pictures of celebrities with wrinkles, it's kind of comforting.

The receptionist totters across in stiletto heels, and sits next to me, crossing her long shiny legs neatly at the ankles. I am finding it difficult to concentrate on what she is saying as I can't take my eyes off those legs. I start to focus at the point where she is telling me all the things I can't do following the whitening procedure, which she reads from a list attached to a clipboard. If I'd known I could not have a smoke or anything 'brown' for twenty-four hours I sure as hell wouldn't have come. No coffee, no tea, no beer, no red wine, smokes or burgers.

'I hope I have explained everything to your satisfaction.'

'I have unfortunately had second thoughts,' I tell her in my meekest voice.

'That's fine Mr Goodbody, but you'll have to pay the ninety-nine pounds due to it being a last minute cancellation. It is company policy.'

'Suppose I'd better proceed with it then,' I tell her, but at least feel better about myself knowing I now have no option but to proceed, and my conscience knows I did try to get out of it.

I follow her up a narrow staircase, while watching her legs and the swing of her hips, to the consulting room. She indicates for me to sit. I park my arse on a deck chair and it crosses my mind that they could have provided better seating for a fee-paying customer. Before leaving me, the fit girl introduces me to my 'consultant' a short, ginger-haired girl who looks about sixteen.

'You must sign this Disclaimer please sir,' she says handing me a form and making me feel even more insecure as I wonder what I am disclaiming.

'I can give up all the stated brown stuff for twenty-four hours but I will need a smoke,' I plead, looking up at her from my deck chair. She replies with a narrowing of her eyes, and in a surprisingly intimidating voice for such a short girl. 'You won't be the first who's needed one when he got out of here.' After aggressively shoving a mirror into my hand, which makes me think she has undertaken to harbour some sort of annoyance with me, I begin to suspect she has a very short fuse. She asks me to study my teeth in the mirror, paying particular attention to the colour. She turns and takes a row of teeth from the shelf behind her. She looks at my teeth, and then she studies the plastic ones until finally extracting one from the plastic rack. She places it against several of my teeth in turn. 'You are a twenty-eight discolouration.'

'Is that good for my age?'

'It's to be expected if you smoke and drink alcohol,' she

43

retorts taking some large white gum shields, which she forces on to my upper and lower gums to hold my mouth open wide. Instantly, I start to retch. 'It's quite common,' she continues, and I don't know if she is still talking about the colour of my teeth or the gagging. 'There's a spit bowl here in case you need it, and I'll give you a few tissues to wipe away any drool you may experience,' she says leaning across me in order to tie a blue plastic bib securely round my neck. Great, I am so much looking forward to dribbling in front of her. I'll never use that expression again, you know, 'drooling over a girl'. It has a whole new meaning. Vile. Because of my mouth being forced open with the big synthetic shields I can only meekly reply, 'Yah.'

'I am going to repeat the procedure eight times with each procedure lasting three minutes.' I nod, as I realise "yah" is about the sum total of my vocabulary in this situation and I don't want to appear repetitive. She paints my teeth with some foul-tasting stuff that smells of chlorine, puts a big pair of shades over my eyes and moves this laser thing close to my mouth. It heats up, getting hotter and hotter as the first three minutes pass and my heart is beating so fast I can hear it hammering in my ears like a herd of horses "herd of horses?", surely I mean a "pack". I don't know what I mean but they are thundering in my eardrums, while I sit here looking like a wide-mouth frog. She repeats the procedure four times, I know, because I am counting. Mid-way through the fifth procedure a tickle starts to build in my throat, which gains in intensity until a fit of coughing starts, which I think will choke me. In panic, I yank out the shields and she holds the aluminium spit bowl in front of me. I see someone else used it before me because there is a glistening globule in the base. I feel sick, and my eyes are watering. She pretends to be concerned, and I can tell it is just pretence because I am used to seeing that kind of thing all day at work, the deception behind a sham smile,

'Are you alright now, sir? I wish she would stop calling

44

'sir', it's making me feel old, 'Let's put the shields back in and I will repeat procedure five to make sure it has worked.' I am tempted to get the hell out of here and forget procedures five, six, seven and eight. She can't get the shields back in, she tries and tries then the silly tart realises she's putting them in the wrong way round.

'Whoops, I have been trying to put them in the wrong way round,' she laughs, but at least admits her mistake, after wrenching my mouth so much I feel the sides will split. I am starting to seriously doubt her competence and wonder how much training she's had.

I manage to hold it together for the final four sessions. After yanking out the gum shields with no consideration for my personal comfort, she takes hold of the rack of plastic teeth, extracts a tooth, holds it against mine and tries to convince me I have gone six shades whiter. Yeah, perhaps, but what's positive is that I sure as hell have gone six shades whiter in the face. While looking in the mirror, I slide my lips up to my gums to get a good look at my teeth and try to convince myself that all this torture is worth the ninety-nine quid I am about to part with. I bolt down the stairs, hand the cash to the girl at reception telling her to keep the change of a pound, and head out of the door.

With slightly shaking hands I defy the rules, open my tobacco tin, and extract the smoke I rolled earlier. I sit on a low wall peacefully inhaling the aromatic smoke. In the evening gloom I show off my new smile to the occasional passer-by but I am seriously wondering how, as a coffee addict, I'll get through the next twenty-four hours.

CHAPTER EIGHT

I wake with the sound of the telephone ringing in the distance and realise I have an enormous headache, the kind that is resounding like an anvil hammer in your skull. I press my alarm clock button and a light beams the time on to the wall opposite. It's nine, who the hell is ringing at this hour on my rare weekday off? It must be one of those annoying cold callers this time on a Thursday morning. I usually tell them that they are breaking the rules of the Preference Service and will be heavily fined, that gets rid of them without delay.

Most people ring my mobile, as they know I don't have a landline in the bedroom. The phone is downstairs so I let it ring until the answering service takes it. I tip myself out of bed and head downstairs to the kitchen. My remedy for headache is strong black coffee, so I prepare it quickly. Then with a jolt, I remember, I can't have any coffee or I will have wasted ninety-nine quid on the bloody whitening. After a short calculation, I realise there are nine more hours to go and the headache is cracking my head open.

I don't take painkillers any more due to a bad experience, in which I ended-up doubled in pain on the floor after taking one. My sister got me back to bed, and called the doctor who arrived with no hurry at all. I waited for four hours in bed, knees up to my chin. When the pain hadn't subsided after the first hour, my sister brought me a hot wheat sack, stinking of decaying lavender. She told me to wedge the sack between my

46

stomach and thighs as the heat would reduce the pain. The pain did subside eventually, but the wheat sack must have been too hot because it left my thighs with a red rash that looked like I had attempted to exfoliate with a Brillo Pad. The GP said I probably have an ulcerous patch in my stomach or something, and that I should have taken the pill with food not beer.

I have to think of a way of getting this coffee down my gullet. After a little consideration, I decide that a straw would be the answer because it's narrow and the liquid should technically be sucked directly to the back of my throat. The aroma of my steaming mug of brown liquid is driving me to distraction, so I hunt the drawers for a straw, but find nothing. Then I remember the cartons of juice my sister keeps for her friend's son's visits. I rip a very short, plastic straw off a carton of 'Kool Kids' juice. My sister will probably go crazy, as she gets really mental about me touching her stuff. For now I don't care. If you have ever tried sucking coffee through a short straw to avoid it touching your teeth I can assure you, it is very difficult. There is a kind of backwash that comes up from your throat which swirls itself around until it envelops your teeth in the liquid you just tried to swallow. Persevering in this position, I am manically sucking, and then trying to quickly tilt my head backwards with more dribbling out of the corners of my mouth than makes it down my throat. Luckily the portion that successfully makes it down the gullet starts to relieve my headache. I pick up the phone and listen to the message.

'Hello Tony, it's Maz. I tried your mobile but it's switched off, so thought I would try you at home. I wondered if you could go to London with me tonight. I've been invited to a book launch in an author's flat. There will be food, drink, and I'll pay your train fare.' I put the phone down after listening to her voice twice, and feel a strange thrill because I am going to get an intellectual evening, and because a woman has asked me out. I expect you've gathered that Maz is always lively and enthusiastic and I don't think many people but me recognise it.

47

I once told her, when she was out in the garden hanging the washing on the line, wearing a rare knee-length skirt, that she still had 'nice pins' and I could see she was pretty well pleased as punch. She usually prefers long Indian-type skirts, wears her brown hair curly, shoulder-length, and tousled like she just got out of bed. I calculate that by tonight I will be able to partake of the banned brown substances and therefore eat and drink normally, so I call her back.

'Hi, yeah I'll go with you.' I don't want to sound too excited so decide not to ask any questions.

'Thanks Tony, meet me at the station at six thirty. No formal dress code, just be yourself, I really appreciate it. I wanted to go, but you know I don't like travelling on my own in London at night. See you later.' Great, a chaperone role but hell, at least I'll be fed and the free booze is a bit of a lure.

On the train I offer to buy her a coffee, but she refuses.

'No thanks Tony, I'm scared of spilling it if the train jolts and I end up with coffee all over my jeans.'

'That's not very likely if you're careful,' I say, hoping to persuade her due to my serious withdrawal symptoms.

'Oh, I don't know, spilling coffee on nice clean clothes is easily done. It happened to my mum. We were at an open-air art show when my father accidentally knocked a cup of coffee off a table. When mum stood up from her chair we could see the coffee had run between her legs and she had been sitting in it. Luckily it was a warm day and it dried quickly but, as she was wearing cream-coloured jeans, it resulted in a large, rather suspicious-looking, brown stain across her bottom.'

'We'll give the coffee a miss then. I was rather looking forward to one as I haven't had my usual quota today,' I say, flashing a toothy smile at her, to which she merely gives me a quizzical look.

Old Maz does look good tonight in light blue jeans and a wispy, sort of, almost see-through shirt and a matching scarf round her neck. She looks the bohemian part you know, like she's involved in the arts. She likes these kinds of events but I've never been to one, and I'm wondering what I'm letting myself in for. I like a bit of mystery.

The flat where the book launch is being held is in a posh area of London. I can tell it's a posh area because of the size of the houses and they look sort of ornate. The flat is on the top floor of one of the large houses and we climb a creaking staircase. It is unpretentious inside. I like it. There is a big oak table, low, brown leather sofa, wooden floorboards, books all round the room on bowing shelves and no television. Before I am even introduced to him, I know I will like this author. As he approaches to welcome us, I judge he is in his seventies and he greets us in a friendly way, with a weak shake of the hand and slight bowing of his head. Maz introduces me to other guests, as "Tony" with no other explanation, so I expect everyone thinks I'm her 'toyboy'. In these enlightened circles it probably wouldn't matter, because most likely they've all seen *The Graduate*.

We sit at the table with some of the guests and other people are standing, talking. Platters of Shepherd's Pie are put in front of us, with a large serving spoon, which we use to help ourselves. Once the food is on our plates, we eat using only forks, which I think is rather cool. Maz has an old woman sitting one side of her who is bleating loudly about how she once wrote an episode of some soap. I hate soaps, you start off interested in the storyline then you hear how many times the characters say, 'we've got to talk' or other repetitive banal sentences. I end up shouting at the screen and have to turn the drivel off. Sitting the other side of Maz, between her, and me is an Art Historian. He is quite old and thin, with long grey hair. I notice how well-spoken he is, and how he pronounces all his words perfectly, which gets me thinking about diction and how people with good diction always seem more attractive. Eventually, he turns and introduces himself directly to me, and without being condescending, he says he has just come from taking a group of teenagers to the Royal Academy. He discusses a painting with me, or rather he tells me about it, and says the group of teenagers had all been studying it. He is so knowledgeable, infusing me with interest that I know I want to see that picture, '*The Absinthe Drinker*'.

'Sorry,' Maz interjects, 'I couldn't help overhearing, but do you know if that painting, and I assume you are talking about the one Manet painted, has been renamed at some point? It's just that I cannot believe it is a true portrayal of what my interpretation of an absinthe drinker would look like. The clothes and shoes look too clean, and he is wearing a top hat, that kind of thing.' The geezer Historian is saved from an immediate reply as the old woman sitting next to Maz knocks a large glass of white wine straight into Maz's lap. The old Art Historian, without any consideration for the consequences, grabs a serviette from the table, jumps to his feet and starts dabbing at Maz's crotch. Maz doesn't flinch and even pushes her chair back so that he has more access. He doesn't make eye contact with Maz, but replies without ceasing his diligent dabbing,

'Well you could have a point because the bottom part of the painting containing the glass and bottle were added later.' He steps back, and appears satisfied that he has soaked as much wine into his napkin as he can as he looks at it carefully, screws it up and puts it on the table. I think he is a very thorough gentleman, but you wouldn't get me taking on that task without asking permission. The old lady soap writer, who knocked the wine over, gets up and simply shuffles off to get herself another glass of wine without even acknowledging to Maz that she's sorry. I watch her take herself a large glass of wine, before she goes and sits next to some artist with paint all over his tee shirt. I imagine his delight.

I move in to the seat vacated by the old woman, so that Maz can speak with the historian without him feeling he has to include me. I am still feeling stupefied by the Maz's cool attitude in allowing a man she doesn't know, to perform an act of gallantry on her crotch. Maz says she won't stand up until the wine has dried, as it's too embarrassing. There are about twenty people milling around now, and despite the sash window being open, the heat is oppressive making the room seem airless and almost unbearable. I don't think it will take too long for Maz to dry out, but I must agree, it does look like she's pissed herself.

I start talking to another old lady, sitting the other side of me, who has tiny bits of black plastic stuck to her arms and face. She tells me she is a poet, and that she had to throw away her handbag en route as it fell to pieces. It must have exploded in a spectacular way, and then disintegrated all over her. I want to ask her why she hasn't been to the bathroom to wipe the bits off, but my politeness kicks in and I keep chatting with her, ignoring the fact that she looks like she has a bad case of bulbous blackheads. I start to wonder if, when you age, you don't care much about appearances any more. It's like all the old people who always have a nasal drip hanging there, or old men with long grey nose hair hanging out that you could almost tie a knot in.

'Do you want another wine?' I nudge Maz, who nods, and I go to where there are loads of bottles on a dark wooden sideboard. I am just musing on why Maz hasn't noticed my whitened teeth when a pansy-looking, thin bloke wearing yellow trousers and purple shirt jostles me.

'Are you a writer?' he asks without any introductory preamble.

'Yeah, mate,' I reply, 'since I was eight.' He doesn't get the gag that everyone has been able to write since they were eight years old, and seems happy to keep talking to me.

'Really, what is your genre?' he asks, and I feel a bit of a jerk for leading him on.

'Essays on humanism,' I lie. I don't know what's compelling me to keep up the pretence because I can't stand

51

fake people myself. I shake my head as though to release myself from my phoney deception. Actually, I could stump this bloke with my knowledge on the subject of humanism, I've read 'the Hitch', old Christopher Hitchens, and Bertrand Russell but I am not enjoying leading him on about being a writer.

'Ah,' is all he says.

'And yourself?' I ask, though I'm not in the slightest bit interested, as I want to get back to Maz.

'Erotic poetry,' he replies offhandedly, and grins, as he can see he has sparked a little interest. This could be because I am unable to hide the slight raising of my eyebrows which, being on the bushy side, are not particularly unnoticeable. While trying not to look too fascinated, I look him in the eye, nodding slowly and earnestly, as though I read poetry all the time.

'Published?'

'Yes, look I'll give you my card, I'm Gregory. Have a look on the Internet, my web address is on the card. I teach writing to women prisoners too,' he says as he fumbles in his pocket before extracting the card along with a few used tissues. Although, at first, my instinct was that Gregory was one of the usual patronizing bastards I meet in my daily life, I realise he isn't like that at all, and don't know why he has continued to bother with me. He hands me his card, which, as well as being buckled, looks shameful, like it shot quickly out of one those self-design machines.

I find myself engrossed in this environment, wishing I hadn't lied to Gregory and decide I want to be part of this world. I determine that one day I will have a flat like this but meanwhile will tidy my room and fix up some bookshelves. The artistic side is going to get some rein.

'Give me a call when you've read some of the poems, I'll be interested to hear what you think. We could have a meet in Swiss Cottage. I'm quite intrigued about humanism so perhaps you could enlighten me further?'

'Be glad to have the opportunity, there are not many of my friends who have taken me seriously yet,' I reply.

'I know the basic concepts but a more in depth understanding would not go amiss, and it could lead to quite a discussion. If you need anywhere to stay, I am able to put you up,' he replies as I begin to think I've pulled a bloke, and, 'Swiss Cottage', what the hell is that? It's like I have stepped out of the world of emails, Twitter and Facebook into something much more cerebral. The smell of books is in the room.

'Yeah, I'll give you a call or something when I've had a chance to look up your poems. I'm Tony by the way, and I won't need a place to stay, just a forty-minute train ride away. Cheers mate,' I say, shaking his extended hand. Glancing over at Maz, I notice that someone else got in first supplying her with another glass of wine. She is glowing, with a glass of red in her hand, smiling, chatting, and she seems at home here. She's much better since her divorce. We all used to be wary of her old man because he would come into the room and cut one of his looks. We nicknamed him 'Evil-eye'. When he gave an instruction, he did the 'evil-eye' and clicked his fingers expecting immediate obedience. We all obeyed without question. Fair play to the guy where we teenagers were concerned, but I did feel sorry for Maz when it happened to her.

I feel like a literary bloke now, and resolve to write at least my thoughts of the day. I've heard that if you write down all the chaff it gets it out of your head on to paper, and as my head is always full of stuff, I might be able to try to make sense of it. Trouble is, my stuff is whizzing around my bonce so fast that I don't know if I could write quickly enough. Then there's the problem that someone might read it and take it as gospel that you think that way, when you know that some days you do and some days you don't. I realised years ago that my opinions change on a daily basis. You know, a year ago I was all in to religion and pondering on which church to join. I even wondered if I should become a Buddhist because they believe in the cultivation of higher wisdom and, as I am already endowed with a heavy dose of intelligence, I would be half way there. Then a few months ago I got into reading Dawkins and Hitchens and my view changed on the religion bit. Now, I think of it as an antiquated method of control, which was necessary at one time when it was thought that if people were made to marry it would help prevent the spread of sexual disease and women would make sure men got to work on time. The institution of marriage, of course, would give children stability. Another day I might be thinking that if I fall in love it will be forever, then in another moment, I think that I might be better off in casual relationships but really I still believe in marriage for the sake of stability, and for children to know their roots.

Maz's daughter has decided to get married, and that's next month, so that is something to look forward to. She met a nice, good-looking bloke at her school, who went on to get a steady job. She started living with him in her twenties but she says she wants marriage if there are to be children which seems sensible as it's probably necessary that some form of control is needed in society, but people don't believe much in going to church any more so you can't use religious fear to control them so I don't know what the answer is yet. I'm against Royalty too, and all it stands for, but then that's my view today, tomorrow it might change. Actually, I really do quite admire the Queen. That's what I mean about writing things in a journal, anyone who reads it might judge me and think it sums me up, but we are all open to change. Then when I think about it, I get all cynical about love being a lasting experience, I am asking too much of anyone to tolerate me. You see I wouldn't want to modify myself, my views, or hide my predilections that kind of thing, the strain would finish me off. She would have to be a special kind of girl to stop me banging one out to a bit of porn. It looks like Maz has dried off as she's standing and indicating for us to get out.

I walk round the room giving the handshake to a number

of people and genuinely like them, as they don't seem superficial like the people who have been controlled to subservience in my work environment. Maz takes my arm and leads me out to the street. It's quite thrillling walking along in such close proximity. Either people will think she's my old dear or I'm a jammy young man. Either way, because of the amount of wine I knocked back, I don't care. If she asks me back to her place to finish off the evening I'll go.

CHAPTER NINE

One more morning waking with a headache, which I suppose is the price you have to pay for over-indulgence in red wine, a late night and replaying conversation as you lie in bed trying to sleep. You can gather from that comment that I wasn't lying in bed with Maz or I definitely wouldn't have been replaying conversation. I saw Maz home, and I accepted her offer of a bed for the night. We sat up late into the night, downstairs in the living room, going over the events of the evening, drinking coffee and having a laugh. She said she never worries about the repercussions of a late night if it means she's had a good time and that I should be glad of those times when the opportunity arises.

I slept in the loft room where Xavier lived for a year and the only thing worrying me now is that I have to go to work, wearing the same underpants I wore yesterday. Luckily I keep a spare suit at work in my locker, mostly because I don't want it taking up precious wardrobe space at home as it is one you'd never catch me wearing outside of work hours. It's one of those cheap supermarket jobs, where the static electricity builds up and, if you walk on nylon carpet, or touch anything metal you start crackling. Also I noticed that, when I'm wearing that suit, if I have to kiss a woman in greeting who has those kind of downy hairs on her face, I can actually set off a spark.

I put on my best morning smile, go downstairs and greet Maz in the kitchen. She makes me a coffee and toast and seems pleased to have me stay a while longer. The sun is already beating through the window, making the light wooden table glow. We sit together in companionable silence, looking up to simply grin at each other, lost in our own thoughts. As we both leave for work, I kiss her soft cheek and she hugs me close.

During the morning my mum telephones, and says she wants to meet for lunch so I sidle off early at 11.45 and walk to town. I'm not much into walking, which is a pity because it is one of Maz's favourite pastimes. I suppose it's because of having relatively short legs or something, so I seem to need to take two steps to everyone else's one and I can't pace well. Mum is sitting at a table outside Pizza Express, the sun is shining, she looks up at me and as the sunlight catches her hair, I almost stop in my stride. What the fuck has she done to her hair?

'I've ordered a four cheese pizza to share and a glass of tap water each,' she says as I approach the table.

'Always the spendthrift,' I think. Actually it was a ruder analogy but I won't repeat it.

'Well, what do you think of my hair?'

'Looks like you're wearing a Jewish skull cap,' I say.

'Thanks for your disparaging honesty my boy, I can rely on you.'

'Would you want me to be anything else? It's called constructive criticism.' I hate it when she still calls me 'boy'. Her hair is shoulder-length, and thankfully she hasn't yet gone in for grey with perm but today it is light brown at the bottom and has this black mass on top.

'I really wanted it to look nice as I might have a date. The hairdresser has really bodged it, I'll have to make an excuse.'

'Yes, I can see that. You don't need to draw my attention to it again,' I say.

'She took two hours to put the colour in, using foils. Then I had it washed and sensed something was wrong when the girl gave my head an extra long massage before running off to get the colourist to have a look. She had the girl put some neutraliser on, which made my head burn. Then, when I went back to sit in the chair in front of the mirror, to have the blow dry, I could see it was bright ginger on top. It was horrible, so I told her she would have to do the work again. She said I'd have to return next week but I did insist and said it had to be done there and then. That was yesterday.'

'You were right to insist, Mum, but why does it still look bad?' I say, as I realise Mum obviously wants me to back her up as she is not one for complaining as a rule.

'The stylist then put lots of dark colour over the top of the ginger, and now look. What shall I do? It looks ridiculous.' Mum keeps anxiously twisting the ends of her hair while she is speaking, and the frown on her face is all kind of lopsided. There is nothing for it but for me to nod in agreement that it does look ridiculous. In fact, I would go so far as to say 'bizarre'.

'Ruddy well make an official complaint in writing,' I say, as I wonder if she embarrassingly came into town on the bus without a hat.

'Do you really think I should go as far as making an official complaint?'

'Yes I do. Make a fuss for a change.'

'Oh yes, that's not the end of the story. The hairdresser said that she would apply heat to "speed up the process" while she was going out the back for her sandwich. So she put me under a heat machine, which had two arms swivelling round my head, and left the room while I was undergoing 'heat' for fifteen minutes. One of the arms came loose, I could see it in the mirror, and didn't know whether to duck or jump up. It came crashing down on to my shoulder. I saw the young girl, you know the one who had washed my hair, widen her eyes in horror just before the machine crashed in to me.'

'You're a disaster area Mum.' She is a disaster area, and swears it was because she spent a lot of time during the first two years of her childhood in a playpen. She thinks it affected her ability to work out how to do basic things. She often can't work out how to do a simple thing like take a lid off something. You see her squinting at it looking all puzzled. It is impossible to ask her to build anything and she has a kind of clumsiness, which goes hand in hand with no sense of direction. I remember when she electrocuted herself on the kettle wire, which was hanging over the edge of the kitchen work surface with part of the insulation worn off. For some reason, as the kettle was boiling, she decided to move the wire by grabbing hold of the exposed area. It went off with a bang, and she fell backwards stumbling to the nearest chair saying her heart felt like it had been hit with a lead weight. I wondered why she decided to move the wire when the kettle was in action as it made no sense.

One evening when we were watching television there was an explosion in the kitchen and then we realised the noise came from the tumble dryer. On opening the door, there were bits of green plastic everywhere as she had managed to blow up a cigarette lighter by not checking my Dad's trouser pockets before she washed and dried them. Then there was the time she managed to get herself bitten by a False Widow spider while lying in bed on Christmas Eve. She is a quiet woman and she didn't call out to us, she said she woke up not knowing what had happened to her, except that her heart was beating too fast and her arm felt as though it was on fire so, instead of making a commotion, she merely opened the window and hung her arm out in the freezing night air. On Christmas Day her arm was swollen and red. When she went to bed that night she found the spider dead in her bed. She didn't make a fuss at all. I can tell you I have not inherited that trait.

Although Mum is intelligent, she can't cook. I swear I want a girlfriend who can cook. She always tried to give us nutritious food though, and just to be sure we got enough vitamins she put a great big orange vitamin C tablet on the side of the plate. Yeah, actually on the plate like it was part of the dinner. It might be my Dad's fault that we never had any kind of adventurous food because he was a boring sod when he lived at home. Whenever she asked what he wanted for dinner it was always the same reply, 'meat and chips, nothing fancy.'

My Dad ran off with his Nigerian secretary when I was fourteen and has two more kids now, well teenagers actually. I see them sometimes, and my looks must come from him because both of his new boys look like me but in a version of quite dark brown. It's quite weird seeing these kids with full heads of curly brown hair, when your own is balding, and underneath the head of hair are your own facial features in this dark shade of brown. It is also quite weird to think that if he's still lazy and lets the woman do all the cooking, he must be eating a diet of groundnut stew, rice and yams. I can't get my head round that one. I guess he has had to adapt his diet for love. He often boasts that he was a 'ladies man' when he was younger. It's difficult to imagine how he managed it, and I don't really want to ask. He probably thinks being a 'ladies man' runs in the genes so I don't want to disillusion him.

'Disaster area, am I? Mum says, after some consideration of the concept. Well yes, I suppose things do rather happen to me don't they. Only last week I did a car boot sale up at the park. I decided to get rid of a load of stuff your Dad left behind and some old books. I got up at six thirty, drove up there with the car fully loaded and it rained, well actually bucketed down. It was morning sun as I left home.'

'You always could pull a rain cloud around wherever you go, and you know your neighbours don't go on holiday the same week as you.'

'Well, as I said before, my rain cloud usually has a silver lining, but I think it was missing last week. When the rain stopped I laid all the goods out on the groundsheet, then it bucketed down again but I had a plastic sheet to cover everything. The sun shone for about ten minutes and after I tipped all the pools of water off the plastic sheet, I managed to sell one of your Dad's old aftershaves for ten pence to a young woman.'

'Mum, that aftershave must be at least sixteen years old.'

'Oh yes, I suppose it must. Anyway, after I got the ten pence, I needed the toilet only it was one of those toilets where you have to put twenty pence in the slot in the door. So I made a loss of ten pence on top of the entrance fee.'

'Man, I still can't believe you sold an aftershave that old,' I say, with a feeling something like sick horror as I imagine the poor bloke who slaps the aftershave on, having to dance round the room as it starts corroding his skin.

'I didn't think of it, I was just having a clear out. Anyway my boy, any luck on the dating front lately?'

'I did go to a speed-dating thing with old Cheddar, but it was a bit of a disaster. There were about thirty women, and no-one I particularly liked.'

'Oh, Tony you shouldn't resort to those events. What about the girls at work?'

'Mum, you have no idea how bad it is at work. There are some pretty girls but they have sacrificed their personalities and are much too career-orientated.'

'I think you're being too fussy. You always were a bit too much of a thinker. "My Little Wonderer" that's what I called you when you were a small boy.'

I'm beginning to feel a bit embarrassed by her questioning, and the fact that I am sitting outside with her looking like she carelessly walked under a car ramp and an oil filter burst on her head. Also, I deftly ignored the mention that she might have a date. I really don't want to know. Gross.

'You'd better go and get that hair sorted. Ta for the pizza, must dash back to work.'

One of the accountants is having a panic-attack, curled up under his desk and a psychologist is trying to coax him out,

'Come on Peter, it's not as bad as you think,' he cajoles. I could assure him that it is as bad as Peter thinks, but keep my mouth shut. If we could have some natural air in the building it might help but it's all controlled air-conditioning. I decide to hang around quietly in the corner of the room fascinated to watch how the psychologist is handling the situation. People hail psychologists as problem solvers, but I think a lot of stuff is just logic. Like, it seems logical to me that someone had to crack up in this unnatural environment. The management system and constant pressure to look good are the problem. Now the psychologist will be employed by the company at huge expense to unravel what appears to me to be an obvious problem. Then, old Peter will probably depart the company in embarrassment or because the psychologist, after about eight sessions of treatment, finally works out that the basic problem is Peter's work environment. Along will come the next poor bastard to take his job. That's why I don't believe in all that control bollocks. I always put on an appearance, to management, that I am sticking to the rules but actually subtly break them all the time. It's called self-preservation.

The psychologist tries again to coax Peter out,

'If you would just come out, we can retire to the board room and talk things over.' The boardroom is probably the last place the poor bloke wants to go, it will remind him of all the motivation exercises where they all chant slogans in unison, 'What are we? We are the best. Figures are our life. Profit is our gain not our pain.' Crap stuff like that. I hear them every morning for ten minutes going through the rituals before they fix on their cloned smiles to face the day.

I watched a botox demonstration once, where this extremely wrinkled woman had injections in her forehead and round her eyes. Afterwards, at the drinks reception, one of the girls who worked in the clinic, told me about their company parties in London. She said she had noticed that everyone gradually began to look the same with bland faces and puffed up lips. Even though she worked at the clinic, she whispered to me advising me never to have these procedures. You see them on television you know what I mean, celebrities with their faces all filled, and lips artificially pumped. When they get interviewed they always boast, 'I haven't had anything done,' and you can see they are being fake because they can hardly move their lips, let alone smile. What a joke. I only went to the clinic because they were offering free wine and petits fours. I did try asking the girl out for a coffee but she said she was 'unfortunately engaged'.

Peter slides out sideways, sobbing quietly, and then allows the psychologist to give him a hand to get him to his feet before being helped out of the room. I don't expect he'll be at the next team building exercise in Somerset. We will be expected to stay in a hostel for two nights, be forced to share dormitories, endure walking a prepared trail, paintballing and quad-biking. Then a discussion of the day's events will take place over something like stew and beer. I try to blot out memories of the last event. My colleagues are like a bunch of personality-lacking idiots, all trying to impress the bosses who stand on the sidelines cheering and motivating, while we end up covered in mud pretending to enjoy it. I don't like exercise it interferes with my thought processes.

CHAPTER TEN

It's the day of Maz's daughter's wedding. There should be a good crowd of the old gang who used to hang around the house, and some of Destiny's unmarried mates. From the age of fifteen we all imagined and fantasised that she would be our destiny. We used to talk, huddled together in the garden, whispering about how we would like to end up with her, and wondering who had the most chance of success. She is a great girl and still good-looking, long dark hair, nice figure but most of all smiling, and kind.

She is going for a church wedding, followed by meal and then disco but not a lavish event, an 'understated occasion' as Maz says because they are not a well-off family. I agreed to meet Cheddar at the pub near the church so don my blue suit and gold tie, bought specially for the occasion, to go with the theme of everyone wearing something gold-coloured. At the pub are the groom, his mates, his dad, brothers and Cheddar. We each down a neat Jack Daniels, although I suspect the others have had a pint before I got there, and then we walk across to the church. The groom is looking his usual poised self. The lucky bastard has it all, the looks, the height, and once she clapped eyes on him at school she never looked romantically at any of us again. Not that she ever did anyway.

The groom said he chose her because of her hair at the time, it attracted him and that was where Cheddar missed out, big time, on any chance of being her boyfriend. She had this long dark hair, which reached below her shoulders but one day,

64

in the summer, decided to have it highlighted. I was hanging around in the kitchen watching, while the hairdresser, a gothic-looking woman with scruffy hair, applied the highlighting dye then wrapped the strands in cling film. It took about two hours, then Destiny had to sit there for another half an hour for the dye to work and we were drinking tea, all laughing together. When it was time to take off the cling film, ready for the wash and blow dry, I sat reading in the garden waiting to appraise the finished result. Maz came out of the house, looking a bit flustered, and asked me to go inside to tell her daughter that her hair was 'fine'. I thought it was a strange request, and as I passed the hairdresser rushing furtively, with her head down, out of the back door I could see Destiny sobbing at the kitchen table. She had her head in her hands holding back a cascade of long grey hair. It was shocking, long grey hair on a sixteen year old.

I wanted to laugh, but consoled her by putting my arm round her shoulder. Later, when she seemed to have come to terms with the disaster, she asked if Cheddar and I would like to walk to the shops with her. Cheddar, who had just arrived, made one of his usual brutal quips.

'I am not walking anywhere with someone who will attract attention like a Belisha Beacon,' he said. You could see he thought it was funny, but blew his chance of ever going out with her. She screamed, ran to her bedroom, and didn't go to school for a week. When her sixteen-year-old future husband noticed her at their school, he said he thought her hair was 'interesting,' and that it made her 'different'. Clever geezer.

The French gang, except Xavier, are all here for the wedding. I will catch up with them later to do the whole Franglais bit, which takes up rather a lot of my brainpower.

Maz arrives in her little sporty car with three of the bridesmaids. I am not surprised she drove herself, as she would not want all the pomp and circumstance of a car for the bride's mother. The groom's older brother rushes forward with an umbrella as it's spitting with rain. I watch Maz beam her lovely smile at him, and wish I'd thought to bring an umbrella. Unfortunately, the bridesmaids, who must be between six and thirteen years old, remind me of something out of a horror movie. The three of them, all holding little bunches of white flowers, are dressed in matching, long cream dresses. They have dark green eye-shadow applied too heavily so their eyes look inset and ghoulish like they haven't slept for days. Old Maz told me she was going to prepare their hair herself to save money. Unfortunately, the curls look like fat, dried bread rolls, which droop round their faces, so it is apparent that Maz is not particularly good at improvising as a hairdresser.

Maz is wearing a knee-length dress and a hat to match the colour of the flowers in the dress. She looks pretty good in medium high heels, sort of elegant. Maz's parents arrive. I like them. Her old man was a headmaster, and is a writer and painter now. He looks debonair in his gold bow tie. I once offered him a spliff at some garden party at Maz's house. He was pleased and he said he'd reached eighty years old, never having been offered it before. You could tell he was almost persuaded in to taking a smoke, as it could be called medicinal. My mate Michael once asked him how he was keeping, and the old guy gave a brilliant droll reply,

'Apart from a dodgy hip, asthma, hernias and B12 deficiency, as well as can be expected, thank you.' I liked that reply so much that I committed it to memory for similar use when I am in my eighties. Her mother is a nice lady too, smiles a lot and brings excellent cakes to parties. She takes a genuine interest in you.

I sneak a smoke with the French guys before we go in to the church and wait for Destiny to arrive with her father. I enjoy the bit where Destiny sweeps down the aisle towards the groom, the train of her off-white dress trailing out behind her. The service is a bit boring as they always are. I can't bring myself to participate in the prayer and hymn singing, so pass the time looking at the stained glass in the high windows. I also can't help wishing it was me tying the knot with that girl. She looks so beautiful, although thinking about it, she wouldn't have been able to persuade me into a church service. For now, I am sitting next to one of her friends who is wearing a micro-mini dress and we are knee to knee in the pew. She hasn't withdrawn, so I wonder if her thrill is a great as mine.

When we emerge from the church, the sun is shining and the photographer, who is Destiny's uncle, says he wants to capture the guests in photos that are as natural as possible but that there will be some inevitable group shots. I notice Maz's old mother-in-law sitting in her wheelchair, smartly dressed, with a yellow flower in her lapel, deftly placing herself prominently in any photo opportunity she sees. As she wheels herself in front of yet another line up of people, I watch them kindly part to allow her a space in the middle of the photo shot. Then, in what seems like slow motion, the old girl starts to wheel backwards, and is quickly out of control. She rolls from the tarmac drive on to a grassed area and ends upside down in the ditch by the church wall with her legs in the air. As her son and grandson haul her from the ditch, she shouts at them, blaming them for not holding on to her wheelchair, even though they were nowhere near her at the time. I think this is grossly unfair, as she could have applied her own brakes. While she is revelling in the full attention of all the guests, Cheddar and I have to go behind the church wall to recover, as we are laughing like a couple of Muttley cartoon dogs.

In order to prolong our laughter, we remind each other of the time when the old girl knitted Maz a big pleated orange skirt on a knitting machine. We were at the house when she came in and presented it to her. Maz went to put it on. When she came down the stairs she looked as ridiculous as anyone can, like she was wearing the peel of a gigantic orange. You could tell she was keeping her own laughter under control out of politeness, but we all ran snorting with laughter into the kitchen. The old dear often shoots a sharp look at you from one eye. It's this kind of wary look, which people who are guarded develop. I noticed quite a few people who do that look, like they're waiting for someone to get one over on them. Maz says the old lady grew up in a large family so there was probably a lot of sibling rivalry where you don't get much chance of seeing the funny side of things and being forced to leave school at fourteen, meant she was unlikely to have had the education she would have liked.

At the reception, I am seated at a table for eight with Cheddar, an old school friend Michael, Lobster (nicknamed because of his turning red both in the sun and when anyone made a joke) and four friends of Destiny, three of whom are quite gorgeous.

'Heh, Tony what have you been doing since you left school?' It's the one who is not so gorgeous asking me and I've forgotten her name. I speak up so the others can hear.

'I work in a firm of accountants in the HR Department,' hoping some ears might prick up, I add rather loudly, 'not bad money either. How about you?'

'Nursery nurse, which means I don't get to meet many people so I'm still single,' she says, looking at me hopefully.

'Shame,' I reply, and turn to the girl on my right. 'What about you Jenny? What are you doing these days?' She looks rather tasty today, but wasn't anything to look at the last time we met.

'Physiotherapist, practising in a gym,' she replies as I immediately start to imagine massage and other more randy thoughts, which I try to disguise by giving her one of my beguiling wide-mouthed smiles.

'That's great, but where have you been to get a tan like that?' I ask, genuinely interested. She gives me a hard stare and there is a long pause before I feel compelled to continue, though I know I'm on to a loser. I get used to the stare of women, as it seems possible that I have a knack of saying the wrong thing and their reaction is always predictable,

'I merely wondered if you'd been somewhere exotic. Africa or somewhere?'

'You being funny or what?' She gives me the cold shoulder, and turns to face Cheddar. Cheddar portrays his cheesiest of grins, puts his hand on her knee and says insincerely but in his most sincere voice,

'You are beautiful you know, and I like girls who are willing to make the most of themselves by going to salons.' After watching her virtually swoon in to his arms, and Cheddar silently mouth the word 'tosser' in my direction, I realise I wouldn't want a girl like that who falls for the first bit of flattery.

The food is served to our table and all three courses are good quality. The speeches are bearable and thankfully short. Waiters are regularly topping up wine in to our glasses, the atmosphere is excellent, Destiny and Maz, sitting at the top table, are radiant. There is a lively hum of conversation and, as I look round the room, it seems everyone is animatedly talking with others at their respective tables. The jokes and conversation on our table are pretty good too. I have high hopes for the evening ahead, perhaps the chance of a re-acquaintance and getting lucky.

Later, lots of old friends from the days when we'd all meet at Maz's house, come in for the disco together with work colleagues of the groom and Destiny. One older woman of about fifty soon catches my eye. Actually, I eye her up to be precise. She is wearing a mini skirt and a halter neck top. She has good skin and looks stylish but she seems interested in Maz's father, despite his age, as I overhear her tell her companion that she is 'going to try to charm the old chap with the bow tie.' I am quite comforted by this, as it shows me that no matter what age you reach, if you've got it, you've got it. It must be something to do with animal magnetism, and as I watch, I make a mental note to look up how I can acquire a dose of it. She approaches him, smiles seductively, and says that he looks 'dapper'. He is however, unimpressed and you can see he doesn't want to be associated with her as he stamps his walking stick on the floor, saying he is going to dance with his granddaughter. At this point I think that if a man of his integrity is not interested in that woman's attention then it is not the sort of attention I should be seeking either. I watch the old guy limp, with the aid of his walking stick, slowly across to the dance floor. He makes an admirable attempt at keeping up with his granddaughter's movements.

Maz tries to persuade old Jolly John to take to the floor but he tells her he is going to retire to his hotel room because his linen suit is creased. The man just can't seem to function without his trousers being precisely pressed, for which he must have taken a Master Class. He doesn't seem to notice that virtually all the other guests around him are becoming more dishevelled and sweaty. I step in and offer to dance with Maz, seeing it as my first, long-awaited opportunity to be near her today. She seems grateful, and we dance to some rather fast numbers during which time I keep hoping that the DJ will notice my miserable attempt at dancing, and put on a slow song in sympathy. He must have a perverse sense of humour, or something, as I have to continue shaking my stuff for at least fifteen minutes.

Just before midnight, one of the groom's mates decides to do a streak. With a body to be proud of, and bollock-naked, he parades across the dance floor then stops in front of Maz.

'Apologies Maz,' he says, giving a bow, so that I feel sorry for the people behind him. Maz replies with a twinkle in her eye, 'I'm just sorry I have run out of film in my camera,' and you can see she *is* sorry too. A number of the guests will be staying in the hotel tonight including Lobster, Michael, Cheddar and me. We reserved one room between us to save on the cost. Although I haven't got lucky tonight, I think about how good it

70

is to be with people I grew up alongside, and who have similar values.

After most of the guests have left, those of us staying in the hotel go to the bar until four a.m. for more drinks, and after watching Cheddar do a final Tarzan act of lifting Maz up towards the ceiling, we retire to our room.

It is a bit of a let down to find it has twin beds and there are four of us.

'Oi Shorty, get in the other end of my bed,' shouts Michael, indicating for me to take the foot end of the bed he has already bagged. I guess he chose me because he thinks my feet won't reach his face. As soon as I am in bed, he starts pratting about pushing himself down so his feet come out either side of my head. As he has been dancing all evening they stink and, I notice with alarm, that he has curved, yellow toe nails, which look remarkably like they could do a successful gouging job. I just hope he is a side-sleeper who curls into a ball. Cheddar, who actually booked the room, is refusing to get in to bed with Lobster and says he will sleep in the bath.

'If any of you tossers get up in the night to have a piss, you'd better make sure you aim it in the bog,' he announces over his shoulder. I am pretty worse for wine, and start to slip almost immediately into sleep, until Cheddar re-emerges from the bathroom declaring his intention to sleep on the grass verge outside the front of the hotel. Usually I would be quite perturbed about him doing something like that, especially as he paid for the room, but instead I incorporate in to my dream state, the picture of him, sleeping soundly on soft green grass in his best suit under a warm moonlit sky.

CHAPTER ELEVEN

On the day of the wedding, I had a brief chat with an old mate from schooldays, Maggot. We didn't have a chance to speak much, so the day after the wedding I made contact through Facebook and he accepted me as one of his 'friends'. We nicknamed him Maggot at school because of the day a couple of maggots crawled up his trouser leg. We had been lying on the grass at break, when Cheddar kicked a dead bird towards him. It was a few minutes before he realised it had landed by his ankle. He stood up and kicked it away from us, without saying anything. When we were back in the classroom, he suddenly leapt out of his seat and started hitting his leg. Then he dropped his trousers, found these maggots on his leg, and started shrieking. The Religious Education teacher called him a 'moron' and sent him out of the room.

I remember he was the one who had the 'gift of the gab' with the girls at school, always managing to pull the best-looking ones with no trouble, so I thought I might tap him for a tip or two. He has invited me to his parents' house for a meal on Friday. I was a bit taken aback that he is still living with them and am intrigued as to why.

I take a bus ride to his old address and dress to impress as I think we'll probably end up going in to town to a club with a few of the girls he knows. He greets me at the front door and we dash straight up to his room, just as we did as teenagers, after a cursory acknowledgement to his mother as we pass the kitchen. The dinner smells good, and I remember her being an excellent cook. I scrounged a number of meals there in my teens but it was not the same as being with Maz, as there was never any real conversation.

'It's like a time warp in here man,' I say, as I survey the single bed with the Star Wars quilt cover and the Sony Playstation. Really, nothing has changed since I was last here fourteen years ago except, I think, he had a different game machine before.

'Yeah well it's home and me mum keeps it clean.'

'I can't believe you man, you mean you let your mum clean up after you, you lazy sod,' he gives a wry grin, as I continue, 'and what happened to all the girls? You can't be bringing them back here.'

'Got stung once too often, I don't bother now. They want more than I can give man. Mum takes me wages and gives me back enough to live on, it works, means I gets savings.' His grin becomes more childish as though he hasn't grown up at all. 'Want a game?' He hands me a controller for the computer and we sit on the edge of the bed blowing each other to bits on the television screen.

'So why don't you get out and rent a place with a mate?' I ask, as my character's head explodes off his shoulders and shades of blood red pool at his feet on the screen.

'Dead money, mate.'

'But don't you want some independence, your own space that kind of thing?'

'Nah, got me model car racing at the weekends, a nice dinner after work ready laid on and me washin' gets done.' His response reminds me of a bit of philosophy I once read somewhere, may be in the newspaper, that if you ground a child by not letting him outside when he's naughty, you will end up wondering why he's still in his bedroom when he's thirty. I think it was when I was going through my phase of trying to understand human nature. Then I realised I was wasting my

73

time as no-one can understand why humans do what they do as adults, except that it's all down to our childhood experiences. What a classic case, I'm bored already.

'So, you're still into that model car racing, and do your parents still take you to the meetings around the country?'

'Yeah, man. I'm getting a deal from a sponsor now, so's they don't have to fork out for me tyres and nitro fuel,' he tells me, with pride etched on his face.

'Your parents must be proud after all the investment they put in over the years.' I say, with a hint of insult.

'Yeah, they are. You still do weed? I've got a stash in the garage we could go out there before mum dishes up.'

'Okay.' As I agree to a smoke, I make a decision that this will be my last joint, not wanting to become a waster like this man-kid. A few minutes later, shivering in the garage, I savour the last bit of weed I will ever do, and the resolve is good.

'Dinner!' The familiar high-pitched voice of his mother, like a dose of tinnitus rings in my ears.

We sit round the table with his mother Barbara, and father Bob. While I tuck in to my sausage and mash I start to muse on the thought I had earlier about 'grounding' children. I try to bring to memory whether it applies in this case, and then remember an occasion I literally witnessed. It was after we played footy at school lunchtime, and he got green stains on his pristine school trousers after skidding on the grass. He was frightened, and said his mum would 'go mad.' We were about eleven years old, and when she came to the school to meet us, she did indeed get mad at him saying he was grounded for two evenings.

Maggot looks exactly like his father as they both have sort of round, football-shaped heads bowed over the sausage and mash as they scoop it lovingly into their gaping mouths. Barbara asks about my job, and because I just smoked a joint I know my grinning is obscene and I start to ramble on about everything that is wrong with my work environment. She nods

74

as if she's interested. I can't stop talking, and she looks as if she is itching to clear the plates. Once I finish my rapid speech I decide to chew twenty times on each mouthful because it's good for you, and it will annoy her. Her little grey head is nodding with anxiety and her fingers are literally pinching together ready to make a grab for my plate. I was always sure she was an obsessive-compulsive housework idealist so I take my time, to wind her up.

'Want to go to a club tonight? I ask Maggot through a mouthful of food, and he looks shocked like a young boy who has something to hide, like he has kacked his pants.

'Ah, no, no don't think I can tonight mate.'

'What's stopping you? We can get a bus into town and you can get a taxi back.'

'That's a bit expensive isn't it?' chips in Barbara.

'We haven't been out together for years and, I think it warrants the expense,' I reply, watching the agitation on her face.

'Yeah okay mate, I'll go.' At last he is showing some gumption. His father raises his head.

'Good for you boy.' The hen-pecked bloke didn't ever used to speak up, and I feel rather pleased with myself for providing the opportunity for him to assert himself.

'Trust you to take his side,' counters old Barbara, 'you know my feeling about night clubs.'

'Don't I just,' Bob mutters under his breath, keeping his head down. Barbara looks at her husband while angrily rubbing her hands down her apron, as though to keep herself under control. I am beginning to think old Barbara really is a harridan

'Well don't think you're going to be late. The door will be locked at eleven thirty, and bolted. You won't be able to get in if you're late, and you'll be grounded.'

'What! Sorry mate, I can't believe this, thanks for the dinner Barbara but I have to go.' As I stand, my legs push the chair back and it scrapes loudly on the polished wooden floor.

75

'Sit down Tony, you have to understand he is an innocent. He's saving himself for the right girl. Those tarts he brought home from school were just not suitable.'

'He's thirty years old Barbara, you can't watch over him all his life. He needs to get out there and meet a girl.' I wonder who I am to preach at her, the one with zilch success with women but at least I am my own man.

'I know all that, but he's been hurt and needs protecting,' she whines, and I can see she is almost reduced to tears.

'It's okay Barbara I'll finish my meal, and then go home and stop enticing him to night clubs.' I get the distinct feeling that even if we did get out he wouldn't be a whole lot of fun anyway. He really needs to leave home though. After dinner I break my resolve, and smoke another spliff with Maggot in the garage.

'Where do you get this stuff if you never go out in the evenings?' I enquire.

'The kebab van comes once a week. It's easy, I always treat me mum and dad to a kebab on that night, so I gets out and the stash comes from the man in the van.'

'But what about your mum? Doesn't she guess? She can surely smell smoke on you.'

'She knows I've got a habit, but as long as I keeps me job, and smoke it out here with the door closed, she pretends it doesn't happen. She threatened me with the cops once but the shame would kill 'er.'

'Well mate, I'd better go and catch the bus as we're not going out. Keep on trucking.' I stamp out the end of my very, very last spliff on the garage floor as I realise the reason Maggot smokes it, is that it makes him feel like a man, his one piece of individuality. I don't need that kind of statement. I am a man.

On the bus I start thinking about an ex-friend of mine, I say 'ex' because he has become what I don't admire, someone who can't be bothered to work, a benefits claimant. There are plenty of jobs in our town. The council found him a flat, then he claims his rent, his fag money, and it seems whatever else he needs, to live in the laziness he has become accustomed to. He seems to have the energy to get girlfriends, and I start thinking about why they don't picture the kind of future they will have with him. He'll end up with some poor girl who, by the time she is fifty, will be holding his todger at night when he wants to take a piss, because he'll say he's too frigging weak to hold it himself.

I like living at my sister's house, as she is often away at weekends so the place is mine. I can bring home whoever I want, do my own cooking, and even cleaning when the mood takes me. Generally, well, it feels comfortable being there. I enjoy reading in the morning, before work, so get up early, fetch a bowl of cereal and cup of tea then take them back to bed. I love that, propped up against the pillow eating, drinking, reading and feeling all warm and relaxed. By the time I get on the bus each day, it's been on its journey for forty minutes and people are asleep or listening to ipods but what I despise is the damp stale morning breath condensing on the windows. Imagine all the germs in that, and some snotty school kids start drawing pictures in the condensation. Disgusting.

I've been taking that bus for ten years and, apart from the drivers, no-one speaks unless of course a crazy person gets on. I saw a brilliant comedy sketch about that by a comedian on television. He had me laughing and holding my stomach when he described the moment the crazy gets on the bus, because you know it has happened to you too, well at least it has to me. They always seem to beam in on me, like they recognise an affinity, or something. The weirdo always wants to have a conversation, and you know you don't have to be polite but you end up trying to follow the verbal garbage while nodding politely or saying, 'oh yes, I agree.' You know that if you don't agree there is no point in disagreeing, because a psychopath thinks his way of thinking is the only right way. I can't seem to help replying though, so perhaps politeness was inbred in me. When anyone

77

in the street tries to stop Cheddar, even to ask directions, he dramatically holds up his hand, flicks his fingers as though he's getting rid of an annoying bluebottle fly, and says in a superior, intimidating voice,

'Go away, you are invading my space.'

Once he said, 'go away you are invading my space,' to some poor, bent old man who stopped to ask him the way to the station. I thought he was well out of order.

'Heh mate he was only asking directions,' I said. Cheddar's response, as he hurriedly carried on walking in his usual very upright fashion was, 'My time is fucking precious I have not got time to stop for morons.'

I sometimes like 'people-watching' on the bus to pass the time, analysing the clothes they wear and trying to guess their occupations but the downside to people watching is that you always catch out the nose-pickers looking for somewhere to wipe their booty, then feel disgusted and hope you don't have to sit on that seat the following day. I used to try to read on the bus but felt I would puke after about five minutes. Ten years on the number forty-two, and I've never seen anyone I fancy. When I can get away with it I do a bit of knee-to-knee contact with various women, pretending not to notice we're touching, it gives you a warm tingle so to speak and is really boredom relief.

As I jump down from the bus into the fresh air of early evening, thanking the driver as I do so, I have a sense of relief at being me, a sort of self-satisfaction that I am managing pretty well in life and, I think, Maggot taught me that.

CHAPTER TWELVE

At six a.m. every day my eyes spring open as though someone flicked a switch. I don't want to get up until seven a.m. to get my cereal and tea, and do not intend to get out of bed until then. Why do I have to poxy-well wake up at six? I lie here this morning thinking it over, because I can't go back to sleep as I usually would. During my musings, I realise that all children naturally wake up at six full of bouncing energy and I too, feel a certain energy at six but convince myself to fall back to sleep until seven. Now, I think it is the human condition to have an internal six a.m. clock. So why don't we get up naturally at that time? I can only blame it on our parents who must have shouted at their poor bouncy kids to 'get back to bed', which makes us go back to sleep after our natural waking hour.

Before the world of television, parents would have gone to bed by ten, making six a.m. a reasonable eight hours sleep. So by nature we must be programmed to wake at six. Condemn the television. If you think about it, it is the cause of major social problems. So we have it, that it makes people stay up late and then shout at their kids in the morning. People snack or drink to keep awake in front of the drivel it spouts so get fat or alcoholic. You can't have a conversation while it's on. While advertisements are on, people dash to their computers, and Twitter or Facebook more drivel to each other and that becomes their 'communication'. Everyone starts putting 'lol' after his or her sentences, which means 'laugh out loud'. Banal things like that really do my head in.

Now my brain is rambling like that of an old man. Sometimes I can't keep track of my thoughts they spiral all over the place. How could I possibly start writing all these thoughts down? Television, yes I was thinking about how it is the root cause of all problems.

Television can be blamed for a lot of social problems, because politicians are seen on it and they want to seem popular. If we couldn't identify them, then they could make unpopular decisions that would be for the true good of the country. Politicians spend too much time trying to look good for the cameras too. For instance, if television didn't exist, they could make an announcement on the radio, without having to have veneered teeth, that from next year there would be no more benefits paid to anyone under twenty-five, or something like that. Politicians who had the nerve to put through such a policy would not have to worry about being identified in the street by the masses if there was no television. Also, if there weren't any televisions people wouldn't be able to watch each other behaving badly and so copy that behaviour. I watch my cousin's kids copying everything they see on the box. Then you notice that polite kids are the ones who have polite parents. Children copy everything you say or do. Maz told me that too.

All this brain ranting, because I can't get back to sleep I really should keep a notebook by my bed. Usually I manage to nod off again, but today I can't. What would I do without *Google*? It's funny, but I imagine when Maz has grandchildren they will know her to put on a pair of specs, and go patiently to her bookshelves to look up, in one of her many books, anything they might want to know. If they were to ask me about something, I would 'Google' for the answer. Maz's ex would probably say something like, 'Ask your Gran.' He used to say, 'Ask your mum' when her kids were at home. He somehow gets through his life by delegating everything. I never saw him wrap a present, or write anything. He seemed to have only two jobs around the house, one was to mow the lawn, and the other was to put out the dustbin. She did everything else and accepted it. I am a realist, and when I meet the girl of my dreams I will expect to be a new man, and share in all the household responsibilities. Like I would already know when to get my hair cut without being reminded that I've turned into some *'Worzel Gummidge'* look alike. Actually, Maz's ex really didn't give a toss what he looked like. You have got to admire the guy for being complacent about society's standards, after all don't we all spend too much on aftershave, deodorant and hair gel? His son once said, 'Dad's idea of cleaning his teeth is a smoke then a swig of coke.'

I had a call from the speed-dating agency yesterday, apparently Bee wants to see me again, and I gave permission for them to give her my mobile number. She called, and we set a date for two weeks' time. I'm not sure if I can handle it, or her, but I'll give it a go. What's most intriguing is to find out what appealed to her about me. Oddly, she was the only one who wanted to see me again.

Meanwhile I am off on holiday on Saturday to get some culture with Maz and Jolly John the copper to the Hay-on-Wye Literature Festival. I looked it up on the Internet a few weeks ago when Maz asked if I wanted to join them. When I saw the line-up of writers and speakers I thought I would give it a crack even though it means enduring the company of the Smiling Assassin again.

CHAPTER THIRTEEN

We pull into the sweeping driveway of our hotel after a three-hour drive in which I was crammed in the back of Maz's car with a suitcase and Jolly's seat pushed back to almost full extension.

'I am sorry you are a little cramped Tony, but my knee will start going into spasm if it is not extended for the duration of the journey,' he whinged. Soon after setting out, he began to enlighten me on how many 'morons', 'cretins' and 'imbeciles' were on our roads. He cursed at every car that came close, had a lowered suspension, a young driver, or a big exhaust. Actually those with a big exhaust came in for extra strong profanities. Maz did not seem at all perturbed by his cursing and I was impressed at how she stayed so calm, concentrating on the smooth driving of the car. The Smiling Assassin also looked like he was about to assassinate the Sat Nav when it took us down the wrong road. He threatened to throw it out of the window, but after minor consideration, decided to let it off the hook by merely shouting at it. During his rant, he helpfully informed us that it was 'pox-ridden.' In order to shut him out for the rest of the journey, I just plugged the earphones of my i-pod into my ears. He taps my hand, which is on the back of his seat, to indicate that we have arrived.

The driveway, which is about half a mile long, is edged on each side by fields in which a number of horses are grazing.

'Conan Doyle once stayed here at this hotel when it was a

house owned by one family, and he thought of his idea for writing '*Hound of the Baskervilles*,' John informs me. 'It is a nineteenth century building.' I can see it is a massive grey stone building, standing alone, surrounded by great Sequoia and other large fir trees. You're probably wondering how I know about Sequoia, you know, Tony knowing something like that off the top of his head. The jolly old copper pointed it out as we approached.

'You might be interested to know, Tony, that the enormous tree to the right of the hotel is a giant Sequoia. The tallest one in Britain is fifty-four metres.'

'You are a mine of knowledge, John, thank you,' I say. He looks pleased with himself and leans contentedly back into the passenger seat until Maz pulls up outside the entrance of the hotel.

Hills of the Black Mountains roll for miles in the distance, and in the gardens I notice a lovely Lebanese Cedar. It is a tree I do know about, as I once looked it up in my I-Spy book, after sitting under one on a rare picnic with my parents. The tree, with it's widely spread branches, had provided much needed shade while we enjoyed our food and, for once, we were all together as a family. After eating, mum stretched contentedly, and lay back in the long grass. I remember the smile she sent up to the sky. Within seconds of her relaxing, my father was causing a commotion. She leapt up startled, and started crying at the noise he was making as he started haphazardly packing everything away. He was angrily shouting at us to pack away our bats and balls. Mum had managed to lay her shoulder in a dog turd and we had to go home.

We drag our suitcases through the great oak door and step into a Baronial hall with the widest, ornate staircase you can imagine. It is wicked, man. We check in at the reception desk just inside the hall.

The staircase to our budget rooms is at the back of the building. The lift is out of order so heroic John lumps both their suitcases up the narrow stairs to the fourth floor, stopping on each landing to take a breather. Perhaps I should have offered to help him because he is puffing like a clapped-out steam train. Their sparsely furnished, single-glazed rooms are next to each other in the small annexe of a turret, with views over the landscaped gardens and various hillsides in the distance. Once they have unpacked a few things from their cases, we go to look for my room. It is like walking through a labyrinth to find my extremely small room on the third floor. The view from my window, is the stunning spectacle of what looks like a caved-in swimming pool roof. Maz, with her usual enthusiasm, decides we will have a ten-minute break in which to finish unpacking our suitcases, have a cup of tea, then we will walk into the town, which she says is two miles across fields and along the Wye riverside. I don't do walking apart from to the bus stop at home but am ready to get fit for what could be my hot date in two weeks' time.

Somewhere between checking-in, and climbing four flights to their rooms, and then down to my room, I lose my shades. As I bought them for this trip I am a bit pissed off. Maz laughs, and says that as the hotel is haunted if I see a ghost tonight wafting around wearing an expensive pair of Foster Grants then I will know where they went. I find her humour, on this occasion, to be very juvenile and not at all amusing. I go to reception to ask the girl if they have been handed in but they have not. Maz checks her car, lifting all the seats and searching the boot space, and they are not there. I was wearing them throughout the journey so it is actually unnerving me that they could have disappeared as easily as that. Walking through the woods is calming and cooling. Sunlight is breaking through the trees, the leaf mould underfoot is soft and there are gentle bird-sounds in the humid air. As we step beyond the end of the woods into sunlight, which is even more dazzling because I have no shades, we find ourselves in a farmer's field. The stink of manure seems toxic. I can't breathe in and keep gagging, coughing and choking. Maz says the smell is chicken dung. But John knows better of course, 'It is in fact cow manure,' he says and I really don't care which it is, as the breeze is blasting the smell belligerently into my face and my eyes are streaming. As we turn a corner, Maz points to the offending great dung heap exclaiming that she was right, it is chicken shit and she runs over to it delightedly pointing at all the white feathers poking out of it. Jolly John is trying to be manly and nonchalant like he's smelt odours as bad as this a thousand times. He doesn't cough once or put his hand over his nose. Luckily the wind is in a different direction, as we turn left along the riverside.

I have never seen river water so clear and clean, there are trout basking, people swimming, canoeing and paddling. Potatoes are growing in fields alongside the footpath in perfect rows, but old Jolly knows they are blighted. There is all this beauty around, and he just has to point out the symptoms of blight such as yellowing of the leaves, and speaks in a gloomy tone of voice as though the whole crop will be lost.

'Perhaps you'd better warn the farmer,' I say deliberately sarcastically, but he doesn't pick up on the sarcasm and continues to rant on about treatments that are no longer allowed due to EC regulations.

Maz goes to take a 'wee' as she primly puts it, behind a tree and we keep our distance. After a few moments a dog appears right beside her tree trunk and, seconds later, she leaps out from her squat. Luckily she's wearing a dress so spares herself any embarrassment, or at least I thought that was the case, until she enlightens us that she has wet pants because she hadn't quite finished when the dog startled her. She starts walking with her legs apart so the breeze will dry her off.

'It's not much dampness, but feels worse because my knickers are satin, so the slight wetness spreads more easily,' she says with a little laugh as though to explain why she is walking like a bandy old baboon. She asks John if he has a scented wet wipe in his rucksack to swab along the outside of

85

her pants so they don't start to smell. He doesn't even seem to think this unusual, and helpfully hands her a wipe. I wonder why she doesn't just take the bloody knickers off. Instead, I feel like I am in some sort of weird horror story.

In the town there are bookshops, interspersed with shops selling unusual clothes. There is the ruin of an old castle on a hillside. In the grounds of the castle are stalls of all kinds and we walk among them. I contemplate buying a hippy shirt, which is brightly coloured and hangs over the waistband of your jeans. Also on sale are leather bracelets for men, crystals, bandanas, or even kaftans. We go back out on to the street and watch entertainers, from magicians to musicians who amuse on every corner and people are meandering unhurriedly on the roads and pavements. I will look forward to coming here on my own tomorrow, now I'm getting some bearings but will take the ruddy shuttle bus from the hotel. We must have walked about three miles to get here, Maz definitely underestimated when she said it was only two.

Maz wants to look at The Alternative Festival before we go to the main festival site. This is full of hippies with flowers in their hair. Organic vegetarian food is being cooked, and live folk music lilts in the air. John is obviously uneasy amongst the peaceful hippy set.

'We are out of place here,' he mutters to Maz.

'Speak for yourself you old bore,' I mumble back.

'Did I hear you being rude young man?'

'I asked if your feet were sore, old chap,' I reply and he huffs at me.

'Come on, you've had a glance Tony, you can come back whenever you like during the week, let's go on to show you the actual festival, it's so exciting,' Maz interjects diplomatically. I find it rather tedious that John can't treat me as an equal adult. I'll blow his head off with my intellect tonight, over our meal, after we've seen our first speaker, who is right up my street and John's too, a philosopher called A. C. Grayling.

Maz is right about the main festival being an exciting place. There are huge white marquees spaced round a central grassed area where there are deckchairs printed with Penguin book designs. People are chilling out over the lawn, resting and reading. At a glance, women seem to have paperback books, men going more for the electronic readers. There are raised walkways with green felt covering them, and fascinating embellished banners swaying from poles in each corner of the complex. Man, the whole scene is one of peace. You can buy sheep milk multi-flavoured ice-cream, fruit, books, coffee, and all kinds of food. I am impressed with the pottery stall, butterfly garden and Aussie bar. We stop for a coffee in a marquee where the 'Artists Only' cafe is separated from our unimportant person's cafe by a wooden trellis. You can look through the trellis to peruse the VIP's, sitting at tables adorned with fancy flowers, although they appear to have to put up with the same blue plastic tablecloths as us. For a moment, I can't help hoping their coffee cups get as stuck to the plastic as ours do, so that there is not such a differential between us. I see a famous comedienne speaking to a group of younger people, probably sycophants, as they do nothing but nod emphatically. I can't stand sycophants.

We stand in the queue for half an hour before the event as Maz says we'll get the best seats. It gets quite cosy as the queue closes in, and I can see everyone is surreptitiously scanning faces to see if they can spot someone famous. I start to wonder if I can ever be mistaken for someone in the dubious higher echelons. An official, wearing a yellow jacket, tears off our ticket stubs and we dash into the mammoth marquee, which must seat over one thousand people. Maz heads nimbly up a large flight of steps right towards the back,

'When we came here in the past Tony,' says Jolly John as he rushes with panting breath up the steps beside me, 'we worked out, that you get a good view from the back, and also that you can escape if the talk begins to veer on the tedious side.' I think it is ridiculous to have waited half an hour to sit at the back.

The green plastic seats flick down, and John insists on sitting at the end of a row so we have to keep standing to let people in to access the other seats, which gets bloody annoying. As I am sitting at the third seat in, I have a skinny, scruffy bloke sitting next to me who is fidgeting and picking his nose. It is worrying me about where he will wipe anything he extracts from his large hooter. He stinks too, like a subtler version of the dung heap we walked past. Ah good, he just ate a bogey, so I can be consoled with the thought that if he has a partiality for ingesting them, at least I won't have to worry that there will be a green slime job stuck to my rucksack.

Grayling comes on stage and launches straight into his talk. He is humorous, I am engrossed, and keeping mental notes ready for tonight at the meal. The three-quarters of an hour fly by, and I notice that the whole talk is being filmed for Sky Arts so I should be able to catch it again on the laptop, if I can get a connection. So far my phone won't work. There seems to be no signal anywhere on the site, which will be annoying as I haven't been out of communication range before.

Following a break of some fifty minutes, we queue to see Oliver James, a psychologist, who is also very interesting. He tells us about childhood and how the formative first seven years are crucial to how we deal with things in adulthood. From my interpretation, I gather that he thinks only ten per cent of adults are 'comfortable in their skin.' I reckon to being one of them.

CHAPTER FOURTEEN

The dining room in the hotel is huge and I know I keep using that description in relation to this place but it really is huge. It has wood-panelled walls and a ceiling that must be twenty feet high, and on the far wall is the biggest fireplace I have ever seen. The window, overlooking the grounds is floor to ceiling height. The three of us are showered, clean and smiling, ready for the evening ahead. A delightfully good-looking, French-sounding, waitress serves the food and wine to us. I am going to be looking for an opportunity to speak to her later about my experiences in Paris.

'In the light of you having read Hitchens and Dawkins, how do you rate Grayling, Tony?'

'I thought he was opinionated and out of order, John.' I say, as he glares at me with what looks like two laser beams shooting from his eyes, ready to bore through my skull. This is just the reaction I anticipated with my false opinion. I am deliberately being contrary to what he expects of me in order to get a good argument going.

'But I thought you agreed with his principles, you being an atheist......'

'I might just take up the Bible again, having heard Grayling.'

'You're being deliberately provocative, Tony. Grayling said something along the lines of, "Moses was a prolific writer both, during his life, and after his death", how can you consider the Bible to be a basis of truth after hearing that?'

'It was his opinion of Mary Whitehouse I didn't like.' I slam my heavy knife down on to the table for emphasis, and the sound resounds round the room. Several other diners look towards our table.

'You're not old enough to remember Mary Whitehouse.'

'Ah, but I know from my mother that she tried to protect children from cartoons like *'Tom and Jerry'* which were, what Whitehouse thought, the basis of all evil in society.'

'So what exactly didn't you like about what he said?' Maz appeals to me all wide-eyed in an attempt to deflect my attempt to wind the old man up.

'It was my interpretation that he insinuated everyone should do whatever they like, and that Whitehouse hadn't heard of the 'off' button on the television. Perhaps the poor old girl felt obliged to monitor what was on the television for the good of the nation. If everyone had the intellect of you, me, and Grayling,' I say, pointing my finger at only Maz and me, deliberately missing John out in the mention of intellect, 'then I could agree that people would have the sense not to be influenced by television but you know that it is not the case.'

'But what has this got to do with the subject of atheism? Just because he put in a line about Mary Whitehouse, you are prepared to exclude everything else he put forward in his argument. You really should include all angles in your argument, if you expect me to believe you are about to become a Bible reader, young man,' John says, as I notice his eyebrows knotting together in the middle.

'You were a copper John, so you know for a fact that children copy the images they see, so we can't tolerate such a liberal attitude. Children must be protected. Violent crime is increasing all the time and it is down to that box, and the lax attitude of parents. They either send the kids out on the street so they are not bothered by them while watching it, or they sit the kids in front of it like little zombies.' I am pleased with my argument and in my excitement spittle starts to form at the corners of my mouth. Maz is nodding,

'I have to say I agree with you Tony, about the influence of television. Don't you think so John?' I am happy I've got the old man's back up and before he's able to formulate a reply to Maz, I think it an appropriate moment to stand, in order to slowly slip off my jacket, to really confuse him. I grin broadly, and sigh, as I flashily reveal my new tee shirt. Written across the front in large black letters are the words, '*A Dawkins a day keeps God away*!' I seem to have achieved a good defeat as he puts his elbows on the arms of his chair and exhales, as I continue my rant,

'You must agree with the psychologist, John, that children learn their life traits in their first seven years. Therefore, it is characters like Mary Whitehouse, who championed on their behalf, to whom people should have listened. She tried to guard the morals of all citizens, and even worked against violent films being shown. She couldn't have just "hit the off switch" or she wouldn't have known what she was working against. According to my mum, she was tireless in her work and several were banned, as were some songs Whitehouse heard on Radio One. She decided they were immoral and were eventually forbidden from being played. Man, I think she must have been a brilliant old woman.' John leans across the table, and responds angrily in a voice as low as he can make it, because he appears embarrassed that we are drawing attention to ourselves.

'You can't take away freedom of expression. It takes a lot more social thought and intervention, you can't clean-up society by merely imposing censorship bans in the manner you think Whitehouse did. Personally I would put errant people in a compound and hose them down.' He sits back in his chair, with a loud sigh, as though he has over-exerted himself.

'She wasn't just trying to 'clean up' John, she was trying to prevent the moral decline that you quite clearly see today.' I am really going for the jugular here and enjoying it, the old bastard *will* stop treating me like a kid with no brains.

'I agreed with the psychologist that it would be good to pay mothers to stay at home in the formative years to look after their own children,' says Maz who appears desperate to take the heat out of our discussion, 'and I'm sure he is right, that whatever befalls you during your adult life is dealt with according to the set of traits you developed as a child, you know, what they call your coping strategies. For instance, when I was a child we didn't have many toys and I am sure that the trait for not being very materialistic was instilled in me.'

'How can, "not having many toys" instil that belief in you? There would have to be more to it than that, to give you a life-long non-materialistic attitude,' John retorts angrily to Maz, and I sit back in my chair pleased to have initiated this debate, which I can tell is getting heated between them. Hopefully he will storm off up to his room and leave Maz to me. She sits thoughtfully for a moment before replying,

'Okay, John, I'll give you an example, my birthday, as you know is in September so we were usually able to hold my parties outside in the garden. This was ideal for the party game my father devised. All the children were asked to collect the long, hard stalks from the lawn that Dad's lawnmower had not picked up. He said that the child who could collect the most stalks would be the winner of the game. We picked as many stalks as we could and the prize was his praise. That's what I mean, why do children have to be given so much in the way of possessions, which in the end they will forget about? I've never forgotten that party game.'

'That's a good point Maz, but I would like to go back to Tony and ask him when he became a moralist.' John is a bit red in the face, and leaning menacingly towards me. A horrible image of him in a uniform and me in a cell undergoing his investigation invades my brain. I need the rest of this holiday to go well so I will start to let him off the hook for now.'

'I don't need to become a moralist, I have natural moral principles,' I say.

'You call dope-smoking morally acceptable?'

'You'll be glad to know John, that I dropped that habit a while ago, so for the moment there is nothing to reproach me for. But do you fancy one of your favourite large cigars out by the front of the hotel? I'll get you a Jack Daniels at the same time.'

As I stand at the bar waiting to be served, I consider what Maz said about coping strategies coming from the traits learned in childhood. Her younger sister died when we were all about sixteen. When I look back on it, we all carried on as normal while she must have being going through some sort of hell. I wonder what traits she used, isn't there something like four thousand human traits according to Allport the ancient psychologist? I read that somewhere.

Maz took her own daughter to a college interview two days after her sister died. I remember it because, when they got back, Maz said that the college tutor, who taught Sociology, told Maz not to let her daughter study that subject. When they showed their surprise he said that as they obviously got on well, as a mother and daughter, the study of sociology had the potential to change that good relationship. At the time I thought 'wow what a guy, doing himself out of a good student on high principles', I like that kind of attitude.

'Can I help you?' I am brought back to awareness by a smart old gent serving behind the bar.

'A Panatella cigar, a double JD with ice, and two medium glasses of house red, please.' I decide it is worth splashing out tonight, especially on the Panatella as it might mellow the pedantic old bastard for the rest of the evening.

Outside, in front of the hotel are five wooden-slatted bench seats with curved backs, which are quite comfortable, seating three people on each seat. I sit with Maz, and people come and go, either nodding politely or passing a bit of time in conversation with us. A large stag beetle walks across the

93

paved foyer in front of us, and Maz says some superstitious people believe that if a stag beetle is crushed it will rain. Luckily, it takes off and its wings sound like those wind-up chattering teeth you get in a Christmas cracker. I watch it fly off into the distance, marvelling at its capabilities. Suddenly it takes a reroute and flies back, noisily buzzing around us and generally making me feel uneasy. I start to flap my hands to keep it from coming too close.

'For goodness sake, Tony,' says Jolly, 'it won't hurt you, it is just looking for a pile of "you know what" to land on.'

'Oh that's okay then, it's obviously found what it was looking for,' I say, just as he realises it has landed on his head. As Maz and I start laughing, he can't help but laugh with us, and I realise that perhaps the solid copper has a little bit of flexibility after all.

I look at my watch as I visit the bar for the third time, and it is already eleven, the evening is passing quickly. When I return with the drinks, there is a girl of about seventeen sitting next to John. She has an array of nose piercings, blonde hair extensions and a big pout. She tells us she is from Essex and I can say it is not hard to tell. She is not my type but I feel attracted by the enthusiasm she is spouting off about the festival. She didn't originally come for the festival she says, but with her aunt to visit relatives in Wales. They found this hotel and booked themselves in to one of the dormitories, as it is cheap accommodation. I feel mildly sorry for the other occupants of the dorm when she tells us that they fell in drunk after three-thirty in the morning, having been to see a concert followed by drinking at the late bars in town. She says they have worked out a 'scam' to get free tickets for some of the events. Then she tries to amuse us by saying that she and her aunt once decided to have a cheese and wine party in which they asked the guests to bring a bottle.

'We worked out in advance, that guests would all bring good stuff to outdo each other, so we bought twelve bottles of cheap Spanish plonk. When they came with the good stuff we salted it away and served the plonk with the cheese all evening. Now we have a rack of good wine, which will keep. Ha ha, ha,' she honks with laughter, while kicking her leg out. She manages to alternately swig a beer, and smoke a cigarette while telling us her story. I am quite impressed at her multi-tasking but worried she might snort out one of her nose rings. I am less impressed with her having the nerve to dupe good friends. I start to think again about 'traits' and, as I start to muse on these, the hotel manager comes outside and starts to call owls, by mimicking their sounds through cupped hands. The owls respond, coming in closer as they call back. It is midnight.

CHAPTER FIFTEEN

I enjoyed that first evening because of the heated, intelligent debate, and being able to sit outside the hotel until very late. I don't often get the chance to debate, and although I won't tell him this, it was enjoyable that John came back at me with such intensity, most people would back off when they realise what a mental powerhouse they are dealing with. As the evening closed in, and darkness descended, the trees became like tall, dark statues silhouetted against the night sky and as the owls called back, getting closer and closer, it was pretty eerie. We had conversations with people entering and leaving the hotel as we just sat outside taking in the evening air.

Every day we have walked across the fields and along the Wye Valley riverside to the festival site. I intended to take the shuttle bus, but found myself enjoying the walk and have learnt to pick up quite a pace. We have been to many lectures and they have been interesting. Each evening we have repeated the experience of sitting outside after dinner, and enjoyed the companionship and conversation of various artists, musicians and actors.

Tonight is Friday, it is our last night, and I can't remember a time when I have felt so chilled-out, tanned and good-looking. It was weird, when I looked in the mirror after my shower, and noticed that my visage (that's a word I learned in Paris) has taken on a whole new je ne sais quoi and I hope you are suitably impressed, that old Tony is beginning his voyage into the

French language. I bought some khaki-coloured linen trousers today, to make a change from the Jeans I usually wear. I put them on, and top off the look with a short-sleeved white shirt, open at the neck. After appraising myself in the full-length, decaying, spotted mirror attached to the wardrobe door and head off down to dinner. We have decided to celebrate tonight with a bottle of champagne, and because John and Maz have been back to the hotel each year, and regularly eat in the restaurant, the chef says we can choose anything we like for him to cook and not from the menu, literally anything we like. We all choose fish, heavily persuaded by John,

'You really should choose fish to compliment the champagne. You simply cannot drink it with red meat or chicken.' I nod heartily, and don't intend to argue with him at all this evening, although I suspect he secretly enjoys the debating as much as I do. In fact, I decide I will go as far as rescinding my whole barney from the first evening,

'I've had time to think John, and I agree with you, I liked old A. C. Grayling's argument for atheism which seemed to centre on that statement about Moses being a prolific writer both during his life and after it. That is a pretty funny observation if you think about it.'

'Glad you think so Tony, and I had time to consider that the other night I am sure you were being deliberately obtuse....' He is winding me up again. Unfortunately for him, he is repeating his mistake of talking to me like I'm a teenager and my old sarcastic impulse is straining to get out.

'He got a lot of applause for his observation, amongst his middle-class, typically English, audience,' I reply.

'Are you daring to sneer at the class of people who attend literary festivals?'

John rubs his hand over his silver hair, holding on to the back of his head like he needs to keep his thoughts in place. Here we go, falling into an unintentional debate. Great, so I may as well keep it going,

'Well, I haven't seen many shades of brown here, which quite unnerves me. As you know, John, I like diversity, and imagine a day when there will be no boundaries, and all countries will be populated by a non-warring mix of cultures.'

'I've had this argument with you before, culture mixes don't work, nobody knows their roots, and people don't know where they belong,' he replies in a slow, deliberate manner as though he wants to assassinate me.

'That's middle-class bullshit John. What do you reckon Maz? You're keeping very quiet.

'I think, most of all, people need a sound background, need to know where they belong,' she says, gazing into the distance. 'It's one of the reasons I don't move house, so my children and hopefully grandchildren, when they come along, can visit a home they feel familiar with. All their memories will be there,' she hedges, not really coming down on the side of either of us.

'Yeah, I suppose all us kids who visited your house and were welcomed by you have those memories too.' I get her point, and realise that my diversionary tactic of putting a question to her has successfully stopped the argument, which was likely to have become too intense for this last evening.

'I also believe in truth, Tony. I am not keen on evasive people,' she gives a little cough, and continues, 'evasion shows you are ashamed of something. It is good for people to know they can be accepted for whatever they do, or for whatever opinion they have, that is truthful communication. There's nothing worse than listening to someone giving you a load of lies, and you knowing they are lying and pretending to accept it. I always feel like saying, in those circumstances, "you keep telling me that, and I'll keep pretending to believe you", do you know what I mean?' I understand her subtle point about truthful communication, and feel a bit ashamed of deliberately confusing John that first night. I don't want to outwardly admit it though, so throw back a question to her.

98

'Is that why you never laid down the law about Cheddar's swearing and some of our bad behaviour?' As I ask her the question it begins to dawn on me about authenticity and perhaps adopting a bit more tolerance into my life.

'Yes, at least he was being his authentic self and I thought that eventually he would work it out that if *we* weren't swearing he might want to adapt his own behaviour, and of course it worked didn't it? To a degree,' she says dismissively. I used to wonder how she didn't lose her temper or try to control us. She would pick up a newspaper, and sit in a corner while we created mayhem trying to outdo each other. Then I remember, as we grew older we calmed down, and often sat with her having interesting conversations. One night, she let us burn different coloured candles, one after the other, which we placed in the neck of a bottle. We watched the wax run down the outside of the glass creating multi-coloured layers which formed interesting shapes. We must have all been around eighteen, and she let us have a beer that night. We talked about our dreams and ambitions but before we left she said, 'I challenge you all to write a poem when you get home, about tonight, and what you think you will do in the future,' and do you know, we all wrote one. She says she still has them. One of us, and I won't say who, wrote a one-liner, which was, '*Bollocks*' by .... He was not known for his writing or communication skills but at least he handed in a one-word poem and even spelt it correctly. I was impressed. The other poems were all well thought out.

None of us have gone on to do the jobs or things we dreamt about that night but we captured our dreams in poetry, and as we are all now only thirty there is still time. We wrote them when we had just finished college, and were embarking on looking for jobs. '*Bollocks*' man became a plumber, one an accountant, one a city IT guy, and he had dreamt of becoming a writer living in America, which I think he still might achieve. Another, I think, wanted to be a magician but went on to do a degree in Art. I have ended up in that god-forsaken building, working with bores. More, and more, I want to settle in a room, fill it with books, alk with interesting people and maybe one day I will start to write stuff. We saw David Baddiel at the festival today. He seemed an honest sort of guy, Jew turned atheist. He didn't bullshit about how much discipline he gives to his writing or anything else about his life. He talked about being well-known for his 'laddish' behaviour from when he was young, and how people remember him for that. He said he is a serious family man and writer now. After his lecture, I decided to reconsider the idea of keeping a daily journal, and have now bought myself an expensive ring-bound writing pad.

I realise Maz and John are standing, ready to move outside.

'I shall just request a tray in order to take our glasses, and the remainder of the wine outside. You two carry on without me.' John indicates for us to go.

Maz and I take our usual seats outside the front of the hotel. The evening is warm. John joins us, and we continue an amicable discussion about the events of the week, until a taxi pulls up. John glances quickly at the taxi before giving a warning to Maz.

'For God's sake don't smile Maz'. He is too late. As two old men, drunk to stumbling point, get out of the taxi Maz gives them one of her hundred-dollar beams. They stagger over, and offer me fifty pounds to buy them some fags. I just tell them I will do it for the price of a beer, which will take me all of fifty seconds to go to the bar. They start singing love songs to Maz, with their arms linked round each other. She laughs and accommodates their behaviour. Because of her welcoming attitude, we end up having a very amusing time with them, and discover they are in their seventies and both from Swansea. I doubt if they will remember much in the morning. Other guests, an actor, a painter, and a woman from Australia soon join the five of us.

The next taxi brings a famous singer. We saw him yesterday in his show. He gave a really awesome performance in his starting piece, which was a take-off of a Leonard Cohen song. The song was all about anything a woman wants, so the man can provide. I thought maybe that is what women want, a man who will attend to their every need, and I made a mental note to start practicing that idea. He then did a brilliant chat on how he hates the overuse of the word 'literally' in daily life. Maz laughed and said to me, 'it is of course, literally, one of my favoured words'.

After he has checked in at reception, he comes outside and chooses to sit next to Maz. She is looking pretty good tonight in a black dress, bare legs and little white cardi thing.

'I learnt something from your show last night,' she says, which I think is quite forward of her. 'I am going to curb my use of a word.'

'Literally?' he asks.

'Yes, I use it too often.'

'Well I'm glad you bloody learnt something,' he says, lighting a cigarette. He surveys the eerie scenery, glancing at the tall cedars surrounding the building and the dense woodland to our left. 'Do you get any howling around here?' he enquires in what I think is a rather anxious tone.

'The manager does it each night,' Maz responds, and everyone starts laughing as they remember the impressive owl calling. The singer looks worried and edgy, and I am impressed with the quickness of Maz's wit.

A few minutes later Ken, a man of about fifty, who likes to attend the festival every year driving some distance in a purple camper van, walks jauntily over to us. He has a huge friendly smile on his round face and a barbecue fork in his hand. He says he has decided to have a midnight barbecue as he has a group of friends in tents pitched around his van parked on the lawn of the hotel. He says he has plenty of food and drink, then he looks directly at Maz,

'Hello gorgeous,' he says, winking at her, 'do you want to come to my barbecue?'

The manager, who is a really good sort of bloke, gets concerned about whether the noise and smoke level will affect guests staying in the hotel. The cheery man assures him it will be quiet, and the smoke will blow in a different direction.

'We won't be able to be there,' replies John quite sharply, and the once happy man, sinks his head to his chest and quickly departs saying he is off to get his brazier going. I am a bit annoyed with John for answering on our behalf.

The girl from London with the piercings comes over from the direction of the camper van and persuades the singer to join them.

'I would have liked to have gone and joined in,' says Maz wistfully, 'but as the manager is concerned, I think it best to give it a miss.'

'Maz is right. We shouldn't be seen to do anything to upset the management here,' pipes in curmudgeonly John. 'Curmudgeonly? I wonder where that word came from? I have never used it before, and don't even know what it means but it seems to suit the way I feel about old Jolly at the moment. Now there are just the three of us sitting outside, the inebriated men have gone to bed, the party people are at the barbecue and I am having my first lesson in how to treat women. If Maz thinks it wrong to go to the barbecue then I will respect her wishes, but John replying for us all, when he wasn't asked, makes me want to get up and march over there. I wonder what he would do if I did go, would he try running after me and grab me by the collar.

'You're collared mate,' I imagine he would say, if he could catch me.

Later, instead of having given in to my instincts to defy John's decision, I lean against the old stone wall and look at the scene. Tents are pitched encircling an enormous brazier, logs burning, the small black silhouettes of people highlighted against bright flames. It is almost like watching a scene from a Western, in

102

which you wish you were taking part. I sincerely wish we were not going home tomorrow, even though I have a date to anticipate.

CHAPTER SIXTEEN

I am to meet Bee at *The George and Dragon*, in two days time. I am thinking the name of the pub could be a bad omen, as I see myself easily the underdog in this possible relationship. It was her decision to meet there as it's 'easily accessible to both of us' she said on the telephone. As I haven't given her my address, and I don't know hers, it is a bit of an anomaly to how she knows this. I have arranged to have a pizza and bottle of wine with Maz at her house tonight, so I can pick her brains about women in general. I quickly read a book about the do's, and don'ts of dating to glean some ideas about the process and, quite honestly, it seems it's a scary practice. I nearly used a couple of swear words there that I could have inserted before the word 'scary' but I am trying to clean up my use of distasteful words and, instead, start thinking of better ways to describe things. It seems the overriding residue left in my brain from that dating book is that she will either find me boring or want some commitment too soon.

I bought a good *Quattro Formaggi* and Maz's favourite Cahors red wine. She greets me with a kiss and I plant mine, as is customary, and she has never flinched, on her lips. The table in her kitchen is laid ready with cutlery and plates together with a salad and bread for breaking and sharing. I like the fact that she takes the trouble to lay the table with crystal glasses and napkins, it kind of makes you feel special. She always tries to look nice too with a just a hint of make-up and lipstick, which is flattering to her, and to me, because she makes an effort. Her long, curly brown hair smells newly-washed with a hint of coconut, and she is wearing her usual Indian-type flowing skirt, flip flops and black tee shirt which reveals only a glimpse of cleavage. She is definitely not one of those tarty older birds who fancy themselves as 'cougars'. That's the name the wise-cracking newspapers came up with to describe women who go out with younger blokes. The old girls wear mini-skirts, tight tops, full cleavage and tons of make-up. Imagine if you stay the night and all the makeup is worn or washed off, it would be like waking up, not from a nightmare but *into* one, seeing a real ugly old bird lying next to you. Some of them must have good personalities as compensation, because plenty of young blokes don't seem to mind the teeth in the jar, the arthritic hips, and droopy boobs. Personally, it's not for me, even if she was some rich or famous bird. I don't suppose the boobs would be droopy then, because she would have had plastic insertions. Once, when I was a kid, I saw a really old, tanned and heavily wrinkled woman of about seventy, on a beach wearing a tiny blue bikini. She was so skinny with these plastic beachball-like tits. Her breast skin was stretched so tight all the blue veins were showing. I was nearly sick into my sandcastle.

'I can't believe how quickly the time has passed since we came back from Hay,' says Maz as the cork pops neatly out of the bottle. 'Pass us your glass.'

'Yeah, although I didn't get much chance to talk to you on our usual one to one basis, I wish we were still there in a way. Although it was so typically white and middleclass, which was a bit of a shock, I got to like the atmosphere,' I say this quite loudly, with a rising intonation, as I want to draw her attention to what I do next. With a proud grin, I extract a black Sobraine, from my new gold-coloured, very expensive, cigarette case and tap the end of the cigarette several times on the case. Then I snap it loudly shut. I thought I'd treat myself to these exclusive cigarettes as the weed is no more. Also, there was this guy at our hotel, who I was sure was a film star, smoking them. He had panache, which drew Maz's eyes to him on countless

105

occasions. Once I have her attention, I withdraw my new gold-coloured Zippo from my trouser pocket, and little by little raise my arm. I flick the lighter, and slowly bring the flame towards the end of the Sobraine, - oh the symbolism and stylishness.

'You'll have to go outside if you're smoking Tony, new house rules,' she says opening the back door as if she hasn't even noticed my attempts at emulating a film star. 'There's a bucket of water to chuck the dog-end in when you're finished.'

"Dog-end, dog-end?" I have spent a fortune on the fags, case and lighter. I don't even particularly like cigarettes, and I am booted out of the house like an outcast, I think to myself as I smoke, then dejectedly chuck the end in the bucket and watch it fizzle out. I return inside and she hands me a glass of wine, puts the pizza on the table and we sit opposite one another. Bob Dylan is lamenting indistinctly from her ipod, a candle flickers between us and a soothing breeze wafts in from the slightly open window.

'I've finally got a date, it's in two days' time and I'm bricking it. I don't know anything about her, except for a four-minute banter at a speed-dating thing I went to with Cheddar.' My breathing seems all out of kilter, like I'm rushing up a staircase, and my news is gushing out as quickly as possible. It's almost like I'm telling Maz I'm cheating on her.

'Oh,' is all she says through a mouthful of pizza. I detect a hint of something I can't quite understand, perhaps regret, or maybe it's because she has a gob full of food that she hasn't said anything else. Without knowing for sure, I can't reassure her that nothing can replace our intellectual conversations.

'I don't know how it will develop but I'm bloody nervous,' I say.

'No-one can know how things will develop Tony, but let her do much of the talking, don't get carried away with telling her your life story, listen to hers. You'll be okay.'

'The thing is, she didn't seem my type but as I haven't had a girlfriend and she's shown interest.......'

'As you get to know her you might find things in common and you go from there.'

'She seemed the type who will want to jump into bed and, well can I say this?'

'You can say anything.'

'I don't know what I'm supposed to do. Well, you know, I do know what to *do*, if you get my meaning, but what I mean is - do I take her back to my room on the first night?' I feel a bit of a flush coming on.

'I'll give you some advice, however stimulated you might feel, wait. The urge or desire can be overwhelming, and people often think they must act on it right away for fear it will diminish, but believe me, it will remain and get even stronger if you wait,' she replies giving me a knowing type of grin.

'Did it happen to you when you were younger?'

'Oi, I'm not that old.'

'I didn't mean you were.' God, I am sweating like a tomato left too long on a windowsill, and I swear I must be nearly as red.

'It still happens to me. I still feel desire, quite often actually, but if the person doesn't turn out to be right for you, you're glad you didn't succumb to lust. Sometimes it's better to feel regret rather than remorse.'

'What about experience though, I literally haven't got any.' As I spout out '*literally*' I realise the comedian at Hay picked on that word unjustly, it is a brilliant intensifier, and I am a great fan of intensifying my meaning. I don't want to end up a forty-year-old virgin like the bloke in that film, a laughing stock, I think to myself. The tension in the air is physical, and it's not the only physical thing happening here, my trouser snake is rearing its hideous head. I imagine Maz coming round to my side of the table, sliding her hand down over my shoulder towards the dreaded beast, and then dragging me up off to the bedroom to bring me to fruity maturity.

'You won't get anything from a brief encounter like that

Tony.' God, I thought she read my mind, but she is replying to the question about whether I should go for a one-night stand. 'It's perhaps a wrong motive, to use a one-night stand for the purpose of losing your virginity, it will be much more meaningful with someone you already admire and desire. Get to know her first.' Admire and desire, yes I already know about that one and the desire is not going down. I've never spoken so intimately to Maz before. We usually talk about books, music, film, or our opinions in depth and we bounce ideas around, that sort of thing. Maz continues. 'In my lifetime I have met many men I admire and you could say, occasionally, desire. You sense the feeling of electricity passing between you when you touch hands, or it is something almost tangible in the air. It is so powerful it can make you feel like acting upon the feeling, sort of want to lie down there and then. You never forget the intensity of it. It comes only a few times in your lifetime and believe me it is worth waiting for.'

I know what she means, it is happening to me now and I want to touch her.

'Uh, huh,' is all I can manage in reply as my throat feels like it's locked up.

'Make sure she is right for you. If you want children look at all the aspects of her life. You know what I once said about children being like little sponges, soaking up all the influences around them? Well I mean it. You want a woman who will do you, and your children, proud. Look at her mother, look at her family, if alarm bells ring then think of it as short-term or don't go there. On the other hand, if all seems well then give her everything you've got.'

'How did you end up with the father of your kids?'

'He had energy, he didn't swear and I had already decided I didn't want to marry an argumentative person. To have to deal with arguments and bring up children would have been awful. I loved him, it's just a pity he wanted his 'freedom' as he called it. He probably didn't realise he already had any freedom he wanted within the marriage, and felt guilty for being away from home so much…….. Talking of meeting the right person, you remember when Destiny started seeing someone unsuitable, and my alarm bells rang until I was proved right, and he went to prison. I could see the attraction she had for him, his good looks and humour but it was the company he kept together with his swearing, which I thought would be a downfall. I said to her one day, and believe me, I had to choose my moment carefully, "when you put your children to bed at night he will have all his friends in your living room and you'll be trying to protect them from his friends' thieving, violent ways." That was enough, the seed of doubt, and she stopped seeing him the next day.'

'Yeah, I vaguely remember him. That must have been hard for her to give him up if she still fancied him.'

'Yes, but she knew that in the future she would want children, and her self-esteem was good enough to want better for herself.'

'I see what you're saying, but at this stage I'm looking for a bit of experience. As you know I haven't been lucky enough for it to have happened yet…….' I am still hoping Maz might offer the experience but she frowns, and then nods in understanding.

'I loved my husband and we had a tremendously close time while the children were small, he supported my decisions, I read countless books on childcare, even did OU courses studying the first years of life. We were from such differing backgrounds so he eventually got more enjoyment from his weekend hobbies than he did from being with me. I got into reading, my writing, and literary events, which he loathes. We couldn't watch the same TV programmes, or go to the cinema as I moved on to liking the arty type film and French film. He liked his science fiction, violent type of things, and so loud. You remember the loudness? But, heh, everyone to their own likings, who was I to nag him in to doing things with me. Then of course the inevitable happened and he met someone else, such a pity. Nagging, of course, puts you in a horrible position when you just want to get on and enjoy life.' Oh God, I think she is going to give me too much detail in a minute, and I have no desire to hear about the sex life she had with him. Subtefuge, I need an escape route quick.

'Changing the subject slightly,' I say, interjecting as quickly as I can, just in case she starts rabbiting on about sex with her ex.

'Sorry, Tony I've gone on a bit but the bottom line is to be selective……..'

'Yeah, as I say, changing the subject, I thought you'd be interested to know that I read an Ernest Hemingway book last week In it he says that if you have been lucky enough to have lived in Paris, you basically take Paris with you for the rest of your life, like a 'moveable feast' and I knew what he meant immediately, even though I only had those few days.'

'Oh, that is marvellous I can envisage exactly what he meant too,' Maz replies, a slight pinkness appearing on her cheeks, which briefly makes me think she might be feeling a little guilty about something.

'Maz, I actually quite fancy a life like the writers he describes as congregating in Paris in those times. Even though it was the early twentieth century, and I didn't think sexual freedom kicked in until the nineteen sixties, those geezers seemed to have led quite free and easy lives. There was James Joyce, Scott Fitzgerald, Ezra Pound, although I think Joyce remained devoted to his wife. What do you think really about sexual experimentation before I get hitched?' I shove my plate across the table, put my chin in my hand and look at her earnestly, waiting for her response, which takes a while for her to formulate.

'I think everyone is looking for someone special to call their own, a soulmate but I don't see any harm in experimenting as long as you don't get caught with the wrong person, so don't get her pregnant, watch that one. You'd end up married, with

110

children and looking for an escape route, always think of the consequences for children. Sorry, I sound a bit like a preacher but firmly believe it,' she says. My desire is firmly enraged now, and I sense myself trying to lead her down the avenue I want to explore, but she keeps bleating on about finding the right person.

'Do you believe in the new expression, "friends with benefits"?' I ask. She is genuinely startled at my question, and her hand shakes as she puts her glass down on the table. She starts to grasp the stem of the wine glass between her thumb and finger, distractedly moving them up and down probably unaware of the connotation of the action.

'What?'

'You know, people who've known each other a long time, have deep respect, and who end a good evening by going to bed together.'

'I suppose it happens,' Maz answers quietly.

'Has it happened to you?' I ask. She smiles, and looks out of the window without a reply. 'How would you know if you could approach someone for that?' I press for an answer.

'Well, call me old-fashioned, but I think it ought to come from the man as a polite approach from which he should determine to back down if she rejects it. I still believe in courtship, it is a very powerful thing, a slow approach, it gives both parties time to evaluate each other.'

'So how would I know when to make the first move?'

'Oh, read the signals, Tony. She might look into your eyes rather longer than usual, keep flicking her hair back away from her face, choose to sit close to you, that sort of thing.' At this point I realise Maz hasn't given me a single one of those signals. Looks like I need to try harder, and for tonight, go home and fantasize, so I commit to memory what her fingers look like moving seductively up and down on the glass.

'Come on, give me a hand to clear this lot away and I'll listen to that CD of yours.'

111

Later, she draws the curtains in the living-room, and I put my CD in her player. I sit on the sofa and she swings her feet up under her on a chair. We sip our wine, relaxed in each other's company.

'Can I give your shoulders a massage just to say thanks for all the advice?' I ask, and then I blatantly lie, 'I often do that for my mum when she visits.'

'Okay, I'll sit on the floor and you can sit behind me, that'll be nice.' She comes across the room and sits leaning into my legs. We sit like that for a moment, the music playing softly in the background. I start to tentatively move my fingers, although I haven't really got a clue how to massage. Her shoulders are under my manipulative touch, and I gently pinch the skin below her neck. She leans further back into my legs as she relaxes, so I guess I am doing something right. I dare not move any further down or reach forward.

'That was a good place.' I realise my thoughts have become abstract and she doesn't have a clue what place I am talking about.

'What place?'

'Shakespeare and Co., that old bookshop in Paris.'

'Yes it was a good place even though the floor sloped and the shelves looked like they'd fall down any moment. I remember feeling uneasy in there but I suppose it's survived the test of time, and nothing made me as uneasy as being stuck in that lift.'

'The bookshop is featured in the Hemingway book I told you about earlier, there's a photo of him with Ezra Pound, James Joyce and Ford Madox Ford. I just thought how exciting it would be if there was some meeting place like that in this cultural-free town.'

'We have the Jelly Leg'd Chicken art gallery,' and I laugh with sudden happy memory, of her taking us teenagers to meet the artists when it first opened. Those Monday evenings, when we spoke to the artists, then the five of us went to the pizza place where we shared one pizza and ordered five glasses of tap water. Old Mario, the waiter, must have loved it when we went in, 'You remember it well by the sound of your laughter,'she says.

'I was just thinking I would like that kind of life, meeting arty types. I never disliked any of them, they seemed to treat everyone as intelligent and had no pretensions,' I say, my voice slightly shaking, mirroring the trembling of my fingers. She sighs,

'I know what you mean, this town is all about IT, and big business, which is such a shame. Did you know the original Shakespeare and Co. closed when the patron died? The shop we saw wasn't the original. The founder was called Sylvia Beach and she arranged that borrowers or buyers could get hold of books that had been banned such as '*Ulysses*' by James Joyce and, of course, '*Lady Chatterley's Lover*' by D. H. Lawrence. The building it's in now, where we saw it, was a disused monastery, and apparently, they let beds to writers and artists. It became popular with the next generation of writers, the 'Beat Generation', such as Allen Ginsberg. If you've not read Ginsberg then you should try him. Oh, and of course Henry Miller. Now there's a writer for you, he wrote, 'The Tropic of Cancer' and the 'Tropic of Capricorn.'

'I'm not much into Geography, Maz,' I say, as she starts laughing and choking on her mouthful of wine, and this time I seriously don't know why I've made her laugh. Now she's slapping her thigh in complete hysteria and I am scared I might see a pool of piss escape from under her at this rate. In concern for my socks, which will get wet if she has an accident, I decide to extricate myself by sliding along the sofa, so that her back is no longer pressing on to my legs.

'They are extremely explicit novels about sex, Tony. He was the lover of Anais Nin the writer of '*Delta of Venus*'. '

'I guess that isn't about the planet either.'

'You are right. It is a collection of erotic stories, again

very explicit.' As she has stopped laughing, I start to slide back into my previous position behind her, as it appears safe to do so, but she stands and moves on to a chair adjacent to me. So, that's that then, the end to my touching her. All this talk of erotic literature impels me to place a cushion across my crotch.

'I was thinking too, that maybe one day I will live in Paris but I need to get a bit of French language installed in the brain. I heard a comedian once say, in his stand-up show, that at one time all he could remember of his school French was "le singe est dans l'arbre," and who needs to ever say, "the monkey is in the tree". The French seem to learn English with no problem.'

'Yes they do, and I am impressed that you want to get to know the language.'

'Do you remember the bridge in Paris with all the little padlocks? Lovers had used permanent marker to write their names in hearts, declaring their love for each other, on the back of the padlocks.'

'Yes, there were thousands of them.'

'I read in the paper that people in London are doing that now, locking the padlocks on to the metal struts of the bridges. Anyway, I didn't tell you this at the time, but after you said it was so romantic that people wanted to leave a souvenir of their love for each other, and John huffed like he doesn't believe in all that romance stuff, you walked on ahead of us. He eventually couldn't resist having a gander at one. Well, during the whole length of the bridge he could have turned over any one of those padlocks but, of all the thousands, he picked out the one that had, "I want to have sex with Sarcozy," written in black marker on the back. Bloody typical of him.' She starts laughing again, and I think it would be skilful of me to leave her on a climactic note so she wants more of me. She wishes me luck on my date, and I kiss her goodbye with thanks and add an electrical impulse to my collection of imagery to savour later in a fantasy.

114

CHAPTER SEVENTEEN

The George and Dragon is one of those pubs where you have to 'walk the line' of ardent drinkers and smokers before you get to the entrance. Peering at you from under their baseball caps, none seem able to stand straight, they sort of lilt to one side or lean against tables. A straggly bunch with imbecilic tendencies, and I hadn't better say that out loud or I imagine I will soon be a piece of pulp embedded in the gravel.

Bee is sitting quite happily alone at a table staring at a pint of beer, which stands like some ominous status symbol in front of her. After a few seconds of contemplating her, I attract her attention with a wave, and indicate that I am going to the bar, thereby delaying my actual contact. My heart is thumping rather uncontrollably and I fear she might hear it knocking out of my ears, what with that, and my hand getting the shakes when I lift my pint, I'm off to a good start. I pick up two sticky menus from the bar in my other hand, which means I now have two trembling hands and walk across to her. I know that, had I been in France, I would have greeted her with a kiss on each cheek and feel there is something lacking in my,

'Hi, how are you?' but I don't want to bend down and she doesn't stand to greet me.

'Great mate, and yourself?' she replies. What now? Do I launch in to one of my favourite subjects or wait for her to speak? There is silence between us, discernible and suddenly spectacularly broken by the voice of Mick Jagger screaming his most famous song, from the other side of the bar that some

115

leather-clad biker has shoved a pound in the machine to hear.

'I just got back from the Hay Literature Festival a couple of weeks ago.'

'That's hardly, "just got back",' she says, showing less interest in me than a bee would in a plastic flower. Nevertheless I press on with an attempt at introducing myself.

'I'm a big reader so it was great to see all those authors and be amongst people of a like mind.'

'Yeah, I knows what you mean,' she takes a big slurp of beer, wipes her mouth on the back of her hand, while I have time to take in her words she "knows what I mean", and am somewhat taken aback. Does she mean she is a great reader too? I am rather scared to ask and, from what I've seen of her so far, I rather doubt it. I decide it's probably best not to pursue the question. She eventually decides to enlighten me about her own cultural interest.

'I gets meself off to Glastonbury every year in a tent with mates and sees some of best bands around.'

'I haven't been to Glastonbury, but did the Reading Festival a few years back, and have watched Glastonbury on the computer. Reading Festival was an experience. My mate did a bit of crowd surfing, sort of launched himself upwards and everyone rolled him towards the front.' I find myself gabbling in order to keep some sort of conversation going. 'What I didn't like was when people pee'd in plastic bottles and lobbed them in to the crowd. Did you see any of that behaviour at Glastonbury?' She gives me a long, hard stare.

'No I didn't mate.' At least we have something in common that we've both been to a music festival and perhaps that means she has a soul after all.

'You mentioned Eric Clapton, whose music I very much enjoy, when we met at the speed-dating, have you ever seen him live?'

'At the Royal Albert Hall, from the distance I was at he seemed very small, mate,' she says with about as much

116

enthusiasm as a slug about to emit some slime to negotiate a brick wall.

'One of the best guitarists around I'd say.' I am trying desperately to stay on the music subject.

'Bollocks, he doesn't compare to Kirk Hammett.' Oh no, she's still in to heavy metal, having moved on from that type of music ten years ago I am plunged into another chasm of despair. I start to run my finger along the menu, or at least try to, but it gets stuck on left over congealed splatter of previous diners' dinners.

'I'm going to have a starter of soup and then the sausage and mash. Shall I go to the bar and order for you?'

'We'll go Dutch so I'll come up and order me own. I'll tell you now feminism is me game, so don't get all poncey thinking you can impress me with chivalry, it don't work.' She doesn't look like someone with typically feminist attitudes with her top barely covering her bulging breasts, she's plastered in make-up, her hair is dyed blonde which I can tell because dark roots are showing, her eyebrows are plucked and drawn back on with pencil and, as she gets up to go to the bar, I can clearly see the line of a thong under her white trousers. Even the sight of that does nothing for me at all, not even a twinkle.

While we sit back and wait for our meal to arrive, I ask the question that I have had difficulty holding in, like I've been intrigued since I was informed she chose me.

'What made you want to meet me again?' In reply, she smiles insolently and leans forward, taking her time.

'I thought I could teach you a thing or two.' I virtually spit my mouthful of beer back into my glass.

'Oh yeah,' I smirk back challengingly, and look her in the eyes, knowing very well that she probably could.

'You're a virgin ain't ya? I'm fed up with blokes who know it all. I can be the girl to show you what it takes.' Despite the sexual innuendo she is blatantly giving me, there is still no rising from the beast that rarely sleeps. It must have decided to

117

take tonight off and take a deep slumber.

'You've been around a bit then?'

'Could say that, but they're all losers, give me a prick that's never seen a clit,' she states without the slightest amount of coyness that, I actually nearly choke on a mouthful of cool soup. It arrived cool and is an indicator of how I feel.

'Please keep your voice down a bit Bee, I don't want everyone in the pub knowing our business,' I plead, although on glancing round, I can see that most of the drinkers are staring into their own pint glasses, lost in their world of barley brew.

'Tell me what you read from my face,' she says, changing the subject. It's such a strange question, and I consider her for a while. I see the sad feature of someone who thinks life owes her something. It's the unmistakeable look I see often, when passing some girls in the street, when you notice that they and their kids have indelibly etched snarls as though they have lost all innocence. There is no openness or softness in Bee's face, and a horrible premonition of the future jumps into my consciousness as I see my own children will be born with that look if I take up with her. I actually foresee three little babies' faces all scowling at me, from under their sunhats, with a vague expression of hatred in their features. It makes me shudder. After some moments of pretending to study her face, in which I move my head from side to side and act confused while searching for as honest an answer as I dare, I come out with what I consider a stroke of genius.

'Ummm, I see social acknowledgement,' I say.

'What the fuck do you mean by that?' Her eyes are hooded with suspicion and her voice aggressive.

'Just, that your face betrays that you know about life already. How old are you?'

'I thought you'd say "pretty" or "sexy", but you say bloody "social acknowledgement" you arsehole. I'm eighteen.'

Perhaps there is some hope for change, change in her perception of the world and it would do some good for my street

cred to be going out with a girl of eighteen but Maz's words
creep in to my brain "remember how children are like sponges"
and the vision of the little scowling faces swearing at me
invades my brain again.

'I thought you were a feminist who wouldn't appreciate
being called "pretty", that's why I looked for a more suitable
description. When did you leave school?'

'Fifteen, I got fed up with shit.'

'Do you work?'

'Mackee D's four hours a day and I gets top-ups so have a
flat. It's not much but I've got a bed-settee, a kitchen and share
a bathroom. I'll take you back there after this. It's only round
the corner.' I am beginning to feel a bit sorry for her even
though she is so argumentative as she must have become like
this because of how life treated her, and I think about old Oliver
James and his lecture at the Hay Festival about traits.

'Are there many of you living in the building or is it a
converted house?'

'There are four and yeah, it was an old house but they
made it into flats. Two of the guys are ex junkies, they gets
methadone and goes to the job centre but no-one will give them
a break and take them on. The girl is on the game she said why
give it away for free and get used, you might as well get paid
for it if you're going to get used anyway. She don't make much
though, or she'd be out of there and she don't do drugs.' She
must have read some anxiety in my face because she pats my
hand like she's a nurse and I'm a patient.

'Don't worry, my place is clean. They are all good guys.'

'Where are your parents?'

'They live in Somerset, and no, I'm not from a broken
home and they are both teachers.' She is causing my brain to
act like a trapped flea leaping this way and that. She is one
thing, then she is surprisingly another, from a good background.

The food could be described, without hesitation, as
"inferior", the atmosphere in the pub is damp and gloomy. The

temptation of a good book is suddenly more appealing than a sexual encounter and I want to go home, but I will try to endure.

'I know Somerset from team-building exercises at work. Nice part of the world. Why don't you live with them, you know, your parents, you being so young?'

'Cut the crap. I had to get away, they argue all the time power struggle stuff with me in the middle. I made a conscious effort not to be like them.' She is obviously making a good job of her mutiny, but I see sadness in it, which makes me slightly fonder of her. It is also beginning to make me feel old and wise. Her outward animosity is perhaps only rebelliousness. God, I must have taken in more than I thought from that Hay lecture.

'I gave you an opinion of what I saw in your face, now you do mine. Give me a true reading of what you see.' I smile at her and allow her full access to scrutinize my cleanly shaven face. It is also a chance to show the whiteness of my teeth.

'A mickey-taker. One step ahead of everyone. Pompous.'

'Ah, "pompous" that's a good word.'

'See what I mean, you're a mickey-taker.'

'Bee, you're too sensitive.' I use the word 'sensitive' and laugh inwardly, but continue smiling at her. The second beer has had its effect and there is a mellow glow encompassing me. Maz told me to listen to the girl's story so out of politeness, although I can tell she is not for me, I ask her about her life.

'Tell me about your life then, Bee.'

'I already told you, I got away from my parents, work part-time, live in a flat, known lots of blokes, all wasters, don't want to get married but would like kids. Kids means some love, and I reckon I could be good with them. I like films, don't smoke, but like a bit of booze to relax. Come on, finish that last mouthful and we'll get back to my place.' It is noticeable how she has started speaking better as the beer has taken effect on her. She seems to be reverting to the language she might have been used to in her childhood, like she just said "my parents" not 'me parents'. I imagine her parents correcting her if she dropped her 't's or 'h's. So it is all a front, a show to test my reaction. Sadly I have still not had any kind of reaction in the todger department but it might happen if I go back with her. My mind is saying 'here's a potential for sex', but the old boy is not rising to the occasion and Maz's words of caution are flicking in my brain like tiddlywinks.

Her flat is in a street of council properties. Tattooed men lean languidly against rusty cars, a mix of noises come from all directions mingling into one heady monsoon of sound. The air is thick with it. She punches in an access code and places her small hand on the imprinted blackness of old handprints as she pushes open the reinforced door. The dreary hall smells of piss and is littered with tools, boots, car parts and plastic bags. While Bee fumbles in her handbag for the key to her own front door, I try to stop myself gagging but the smell is making me think there must be a pair of tramps underpants in one of those bags, and I am holding my breath. It reminds me of the time I agreed to be Father Christmas at an infants' school for their Christmas Fayre. Maz talked me into it because she'd agreed to help one of the stallholders. To get me dressed in my costume we had to squeeze ourselves into a tiny room. She helped me on with the oversized red costume, and then there was a choice of various beards in a cardboard box. We pulled them out and she made me try each one on to see which suited me best. The smell, just like in this hallway, was appalling, loose moustache hairs tickled my nostrils, and as there was only a small mouth space between the yellowing beard and moustache I had to inhale the stale, trapped breath, of past Father Christmases. I therefore had to ask the children what they wanted for Christmas through pursed lips and most of them burst into tears as I tried to speak without taking a breath. As I began to sweat profusely, my ponytail, which Maz had tucked up inside the hat, came loose showing out of one side of my white cascading curly wig.

'Why has Father Christmas got two colours of hair and

why doesn't he say "Ho ho ho"?' one boy asked his Dad. So I quickly managed a 'Ho ho ho' before I got completely sussed.

Once inside Bee's place the air is cleaner and, trying to be a good hostess, she takes me back out in to the corridor where she kindly shows me the shared bathroom. As I am still gagging I decide to take immediate advantage to get away for a few minutes to have time to think, and I shut the door firmly behind me. The useless lock is hanging precariously from one screw. Mould is growing on the grouting above the bath and there are green stains from where the tap has leaked into the bath. The toilet, when I lift the lid (and I'm wary of lifting a shut lid as you never know what is waiting to surprise you), is stained round the rim with layers of yellow but at least I am spared having to peruse a turd. On the shelf behind the toilet are various gels, shampoos and condoms. I check the date and slip a featherlight into my pocket. I know I should have come prepared with my own, but it's not something I do, as I never expect to get lucky. After a good handwash, I am ready to face the next hour or so until I can diplomatically get out of this date from hell. I open the door tentatively, slowly prolonging the moment when I have to join her but she jumps out at me from where she has been hiding behind the door, wearing nothing but a diaphanous nightie, shouting, 'Boo'. After I have let out an intense scream she tries to calm me.

'Scuse me getting changed but I want to relax now I'm home.' It amazes me that she had the nerve to walk out in to the corridor, where any of the occupants could have seen her in almost nakedness. Following her back into her room, I watch the movement of her butt cheeks, and as she turns round I notice she is fatter than I expected and her stomach droops over her minge. 'Take a pew Tony. I'll fix you a cider,' she says without considering that I might prefer coffee.

There is still no stirring from the old trouser snake even as I sit, mesmerised by her movements while she prepares the drinks, which she keeps on a plastic trolley near the window.

There is a small television on a wooden stand to the left of the window and, surprisingly, a bookcase to the right, where books are haphazardly stacked amongst CD's.

'Can I take a gander at your books and CD's?' I ask, as I'm already half way across the room.

'Help ya'self man. They're just stuff I collects at charity stores or car boots.'

I kneel in front of the bookcase, and instinctively start standing the books in rows after I take each one from the shelf to look at the cover. It's not that I'm a snobbish reader or anything but I am quite impressed by what is here. Somehow I thought she'd have no books or, at the very least, a collection of tacky love stories but she doesn't. There are some Ian McEwan, Sebastian Faulks, dictionary, thesaurus and even a well-used copy of an Allen Ginsberg biography. On first sight of it on her bookshelf I can't believe it is hers, but then Maz said Ginsberg was a beat poet who believed in free expression, and Bee definitely seems to be in to free expression. She doesn't seem to have the intellect for this type of reading though. Although I am intrigued with the contrast between the person and the bookshelf I can't be bothered to carry on trying for that type of conversation. She will put me down if I start to ask anything so I just wander back to the sofa bed. After raising our glasses and clinking them together, I put mine down on to the glass table. She sits next to me on the bed settee and starts to nuzzle my neck.

CHAPTER EIGHTEEN

I am on my way home when my mobile starts vibrating in my pocket. I am very surprised to see it is Maz as she knew I was out on a date.

'Maz, what's up?'

'It's John, he's looking after his son's greyhound and has got ill. I've put a call out to the doctor. I am going up to take care of him and, well, I am not sure I can walk a greyhound to be fair.'

'You're not making much sense, are you asking me to help you and where have you got to go?'

'Yes, oh Tony, he's in Huddersfield. I know it's a lot to ask you to come with me in your few days off, but would you? We would need to leave at five in the morning. I can't go tonight because I've been to the pub and had a couple of glasses of wine,' she says with panic in her voice.

'What's wrong with the old guy now?' I ask.

'One of his urine infections, he thinks. I have located the nearest doctor to where he is staying, and he is going to visit John and give him some antibiotics. He really sounds bad and can't walk the dog. He says the house is built "a bit funny". The back garden is down some steps and, as the dog won't go down the steps he can't just let it out in to the garden, so he needs someone to walk it. I said I'd go but I am loathe to drive all that way on my own, it must be about a five-hour trip. I've already programmed the postcode into my sat nav.'

'Count me in. I'll get back home, sling a few bits in a bag and be ready and waiting at five a.m.'

'Sorry if I've interrupted anything, and for ringing so late,' she says.

'See you in the morning. Stop panicking.' As I click the 'end call' button it feels good to have a warm glow of anticipation.

'

CHAPTER NINETEEN

Maz is on time. Waiting out on the road for her, backpack on my back, I am shivering like a shaven dog that has just left the poodle parlour. I jump into her 207 sport and we are quickly away. She likes sporty cars, like she had this awesome red Ford Puma before this car. The sat nav is set with a bloke telling us whether to turn left or right at the end of every road. Maz says she thinks the bloke's voice is more soothing than the female voice which, she says she perceives, becomes slightly hysterical if she takes a wrong turn and the machine has to reassess the route. Maz told me that "turn around when possible", repeated several times, just sounds better when bellowed at you electronically by a nameless man's voice.

'Thanks for coming, Tony. I am so worried about John as I know how quickly these infections can take hold. He said he was "burning up and wanting to die", when he called last night. I was in the pub having a great chat with a landscape gardener, who was educated at Oxford. We'd just got on to discussing books, after finding we initially had the gardening in common.'

'Trust old Jolly to get himself a urine infection when he's miles from anyone.' I say, and feel a little pleased with John that he managed to scupper Maz's new bloke interest.

'Yes, well we are all lucky to have each other. You know, if the roles were reversed, I am sure he would come with me to help you.'

'I am sure he would Maz,' I say unconvinced, and try not to let my reply sound sarcastic.

'Well, did you gain any experience last night?' She can't resist asking and glances at me from the corner of her eye. I actually like that about Maz, she doesn't hold back on the questions, it's kind of straightforward.

'Actually, I had to tell her that I had used too much Chamomile soap before the date. You know, it is renowned for its relaxing qualities.'

'Oh, you mean you couldn't....'

'Yeah, okay, let's just say she wasn't my type.' I lever the back of my seat in to a virtual lay-down position, and stretch out my legs. The countryside flashes by and I half-know I should be taking it all in but it was quite an experience last night and the need to think about Bee is overtaking me and I don't want to answer any more questions at the moment.

Since I was in year ten I have wanted a girlfriend of my own. It started off simple like that. I soon realised that it wasn't going to be that easy for me at school, not with the name I am saddled with, "Tony Goodbody". It has always been hard to live with a name like that, especially at school after frigging Cheddar pointed out to the class the meaning of my first name. My surname, "Goodbody" would be okay if you actually had one, a good physique with a six-pack, but I have always been short and a little on the rotund side, not fat, but rounded with particularly short legs. This meant that my mum had to cut about two inches off the legs of my school trousers to shorten them. Unfortunately, she did it to every pair using nail scissors. By the time she had hemmed them I often had one trouser leg shorter than the other. This wouldn't have been so bad if she had at least hemmed them with the same colour cotton as the trouser material, but she always used a shade lighter and was not adept at catching the material on the inside. She managed to sew right through, and I had these stitches attracting everyone's attention, like I had a bloody row of glowworms round my ankles. At school break times I would be out there in the playground or on the field, tackling, skidding and getting into every scrum I could in order to put a hole in the knee of my trousers. She never ironed them, nor was she bothered when I eventually did get holes in them, sending me to school with ragged holes in each knee to add to the aesthetic appearance.

With hindsight, I can see why I wasn't the boy who would most appeal to girls of that age. My appearance wasn't helped by the fact that this lanky boy joined our class halfway through year ten. The teacher looked around the class, seeming to consider for ages, before callously deciding to put me in charge of being his chaperone while he settled in. The kid, about twelve inches taller than me, was so scared of everything that he stuck around me all the time making me appear shorter than ever, so I end up with the nickname of 'Shorty'. 'Shorty, Simpleton, Goodbody' does nothing for your street cred. I was very relieved when I grew tall enough to wear a standard thirty-inch leg. So that's a description of me, slightly rounded but standard leg thirty, not a bad-looking face with full lips, a good smile and balding head. I wholly blame the trousers though, for not having had a girlfriend at school, as I can't imagine a girl would be put off by the thought of having a surname like Goodbody, if she eventually married me. When I made an attempt at chat up they all said they liked me as a 'friend.' But it's strange how that's come around, because I said the very same thing to Bee last night,

'I am better friend material than lover, Bee. I like you and all that but I don't think it will work between us.' She still had her head buried in my neck at the time, nipping the skin with her teeth, one hand rubbing the front of my trousers, the other holding her glass of cider. When she raised her head, at my 'friend only' option, she gave me the evilest stare and calmly poured the liquid into my lap. I left immediately after, with a huge wet stain on the front of my trousers and I was able to sympathize with how Maz must have felt at that book launch. It amazed me how far one small cider can spread. I was walking down the road when Maz's phone call came in.

We take the toll road with Maz really getting a chance to put her foot down and it is quite a thrill. That's something else you don't know about me; I am a quiet thrill-seeker. You wouldn't think it to look at me, but it is true. I'm not an out and out risk-taker all things in moderation, but I think life is for living and I don't want to be cocooned in perpetual safety. I don't want to break society's rules because sensible rules keep things in order, but I do consider some rules, usually house rules, as being thought up by morons. If someone's house rule is to put the toilet seat down, then I leave it up. If they are not allowed to put their elbows on the table, then I take delight in putting mine firmly on the table, and I really don't care which wine goes with which meat.

There are a few geezers at work, who go to the safety of their own homes at night and spend all their time on computer games, on-line, shooting the hell out of each other or watching porn. They don't have conversation, it simply doesn't exist in their world. I wind Maz up about my porn use but it is brief, often just to see if there is anything new to view. Really it's junk, a big money-making factory and people are so gullible to fall for it. If a girl asked me to do half of what I've seen on the screen I'd actually make myself run, even though I don't do running. I am a bloke who likes honest talk. For instance, I like the honesty of humanists. If you look at the list of celebrities who are members of the Humanist Society you can see, apart from the beliefs, a common thread of openness amongst them.

A lot of people my age haven't seen the light yet and I am not just talking about God but about conversation, neat loving, and wanting to stoke a woman's inner passion then bring her off slowly until she is wild with abandon. If only someone would give me the chance. I could have had that experience with Bee but she was acting like a porn star and it turned me right off. Perhaps I need to go back to see her and draw out her authenticity, if she has any. Why do I feel so bothered? I wonder if she has given me a second thought?

'Shall we stop at the next services Tony, I could do with a coffee and the toilet,' Maz interrupts my musings.

'Yeah, do that, it will be good to stretch the legs.'

CHAPTER TWENTY

We arrive in a grey, overcast Huddersfield at eleven a.m. The landscape, as we approach, is magnificent, hills of green for miles behind the houses but in the town it hits you, the greyness. The house, in which Jolly John is staying, is modern and nice-looking, in a new development built into a hillside. John, in a shabby pair of pyjamas, a blanket hooked round his shoulders and a huge black greyhound greet us at the door. I must admit to hanging back as the dog eyes me up although John is holding his collar, which is about six inches wide. That scares me a bit, if he needs a collar like that, he must be a strong beast and John looks particularly weak. Maz takes the initiative and strokes the dog's head and he's a gonner, I swear he virtually swoons under her touch and buckles at the knees, slinking into his sleeping quarters like an enraptured groupie. The front door is on street level but I can see, from where we are standing, that you have to go downstairs to the living area and back garden.

'Maz, thanks for coming, I feel terrible and have to get back to bed. Can you go out and get some painkillers as soon as you are ready? The shop is just down this street, then along the main road to the end. Khan's Corner Store, you can't miss it.' John looks like he is ready to collapse and Maz feels his forehead.

'Have you had cups of tea or water?'

'Yes, I've had water but mostly I've just been sleeping since yesterday. The dog can't get down the stairs to the garden but I just managed to put his lead on and take him for a crap at seven this morning. You'll need to take him with you, when you go to the shop, as he needs a proper w.a.l.k., I should think very soon, only don't say the word 'w.a.l.k.' before you're ready to go or he'll be leaping about everywhere. The lead is hanging there.' He points to the coat rack, 'and you need the blue plastic bags he might do anything up to three shits in one outing.'

'Get back to bed and I'll make us all a coffee then we'll take him out. What's your name boy?' She looks at the dog and he looks up at her with huge, loving, trusting brown eyes. John tells her his name is 'Macabre' but shortened to 'Mac' and it kind of suits him. So far, John has not even acknowledged me but he does look ill the poor old geezer.

'It's good of Tony to come with me, as I don't like driving distances like that on my own, isn't it John?' she prompts.

'Oh yes, very nice. Hello Tony. I'll get back to bed then.' He barely gives me a glance, and I just nod at him. Looks like Maz and I will be entertaining ourselves for the rest of the day and evening, which gives me a feeling of such perverse pleasure that I can't help grinning. The dog starts whining, a pitying sound that pulls at your very conscience.

After a coffee, we take our bags to our rooms. She has a double bedroom at the back of the house and I have a single the other side of a bathroom, which we are to share. We both have a door from our respective rooms, which leads into the bathroom.

'I will lock the door to your room when I'm in the bathroom Tony, and you do the same, lock my door when you're in there. Don't forget, or I might accidentally walk in on you, oh and yes, we had both better remember to unlock when we've finished or the other won't be able to get in again without having to go through the other's room.' I nod in agreement, although my brain is running in to all kinds of imaginative scenes. Me forgetting to lock her door, me forgetting to unlock her door, which would force her to have to come in to my room, as I turn round naked from having had a shower.

'Come on then, let's take Mac out, his whining is getting louder.' She picks up a jacket and heads for the stairs.

'Heh, Mac are you ready for a walk?' she says, ignoring John's warning about not saying the actual word. The beast leaps up from his bedding just as I am climbing the stairs. With perfect accuracy and timing, as though he has assessed that my head would be level with the landing, he swipes out his tail, which hits me across the forehead. It is like being whacked with a long length of heavy metal piping. I cry in pain and sit on the stair holding my head in my hands. Maz doesn't even try to help me as she is shrieking with raucous laughter. The dog is so excited he is virtually pinning her against the wall with his huge black body, his claws scratching the wood block flooring and his murderous tail continues to swish in all directions. She manages to grab hold of his collar, snatch the lead off the hook and attach it. We all plunge out in to the street. I feel a bulge appearing on my forehead, which feels like it could attain the size of a boiled egg.

Mac walks majestically next to Maz, holding his head up like a proud black prince. They look like they were made for each other. She holds his lead across her body and keeps it on a short leash. We take the described route to the shop, and Maz hands the dog to me while she goes in to buy the painkillers and a few items we will need for the next couple days. I sit on a low wide wall, kicking my feet, feeling generally all right with the world, looking forward to my time alone with Maz later tonight.

Mac looks up as though he is giving me the eye, and then cunningly raises his tail in order to eject, with no effort at all, a long brown turd, which slides out with perfection and lands on the wall next to me. I am horrified, and realise with some anxiety, that every wall I have ever sat on in my lifetime has potentially had a dog turd on it. This starts me worrying about, and trying to remember, every instance of when I had the occasion to sit on a wall and where I went afterwards. For the next few minutes I start to manically obsess, and by the time I think about moving off the wall, and away from the evidence, I must have flashbacked to every occasion since I was fifteen years old. I knew by instinct, or perhaps someone told me as a child, that it was dangerous to sit leaning against a lamppost in case a tramp or dog had pissed against it, but you don't think of the top part of a wall as having the potential to be a contaminated zone. Maz, who is still in the shop, has the plastic bags to scoop the poop and you wouldn't get me doing it anyway. You have to put the bag on your hand and literally pick up the mess whether soft or hard, and I am sure the sensation would send impulses to my brain, which would make me start throwing up. I therefore have no alternative but to pretend it hasn't happened. Luckily there is no-one else around to have been a witness to this disgrace.

I glance once more at the steaming brown load, and move to where the newspaper stand is situated by the door of the shop. As I try to look concernedly at the headlines on all the tabloids about the imminent hosepipe bans, Mac, who has trotted along nicely with me, looking as innocent as a crafty juvenile delinquent, also takes a studious gander at the stand. Before I can stop him, he lifts his leg and the day's accumulation of pee is cascading like a magnificent yellow waterfall across the papers. Mr Khan, barges out of his shop, leaping over the stream of urine, which is running down the littered street. I assume it's Mr Khan as he is Indian-looking and shouts at me in what sounds like a mix of Leeds/Punjabi accent,

'You lit bastar, what you doing let that dog pee on papers?' He shakes his fist at me and before you can say "jack rabbit", Mac starts legging it off down the road, yanking me along with him. We are moving at some pace, and I just have a chance to glance over my shoulder to see Maz chasing after us. She will never forgive me if I were to let go of the hound's lead. He stops suddenly, when we get to the next lamppost, to sniff and lift his leg again. Breathless, Maz draws level drops her hands to her knees and gasping, leans forward, her shopping bag hanging precariously from her wrist.

Later that evening, after dinner, Maz and I are lounging on leather sofas, looking out at the small garden through the patio doors. We are exhausted and know we have only two hours' rest before the dog will demand his ten o'clock walk. John has been attended to, which didn't take much as he is not eating. He had his pills and a cup of tea.

'So, didn't it work out between you and Bee?' Maz enquires.

'It's weird. She's kind of hooked me in to thinking about her, but she's fake. It's like her identity has been taken over. Oh and she calls herself "Bee" as she says she's "buzzing". Her real name is Berenice.'

Maz reaches to the coffee table for her glass of wine.

'I am being so careful here Tony, all the carpets being white and everything. I'm terrified of spilling anything.' She leans back slowly. 'What do you mean by "fake" exactly?'

'Well, it's all the make-up, the dyed blonde hair, the swearing. She couldn't have been brought up like that. She said her parents are teachers, in fact, I think her old man is a headmaster. It's definitely a rebellion kind of thing going on. Oddly, when I went to the speed- dating, I actually thought that was the type of girl I was looking for, you know, one who would be willing to put out so I could gain some experience. I seem to have come a long way since then.'

'Does she live with them?'

'What, her parents? No, she's got a ground floor council flat. It's a converted house which she shares with a couple of drug addicts and a prostitute.' I notice Maz raise her eyebrows, before I continue. 'She took me there, last night, after the date in the pub. Man, it's dire to put it mildly. Mouldy bathroom, carpets feel damp that kind of thing. While I was in the bathroom out in the hallway, she got changed in to a completely see-through short nightie thing that barely covered her arse.'

'That's called a "baby-doll". It was thought at one time they were the thing to entice your husband or partner. You didn't find it enticing then?' Maz asks with a hint of amusement.

'Stop laughing, no, I didn't. Am I not like other men then? I told you before, I just prefer natural women, not ones made up to that degree. At least I want to see what I'm kissing and not come out of a clinch with a mix of chemicals attached to my face.' Maz looks thoughtful but doesn't reply. 'Also I don't see the need for the see-through thing, when all you naturally want to do is get to what's underneath. Well usually you would.'

'I think perhaps then, the dressing up is more exciting for the woman. In her head she feels sexy because she *thinks* her being dressed like that will turn on the man. It's all psychological, a woman's arousal starts in the brain, and she has to feel desired before the other parts are ready for stimulation.'

'Yeah, yeah, I know all that Maz but I'm not fake, and I couldn't genuinely tell a woman she's beautiful if her face is covered in that amount of slap. Cheddar tells every girl he meets she is beautiful. He told me to try it at the speed-dating but it didn't feel right. I tried it on Bee when I only had four minutes to impress her, but she slammed me down.'

'Oddly, she did choose to see you again though.'

'What do you mean "oddly"?'

'I just meant that you tried Cheddar's tactic and it obviously worked.'

'So you don't think she chose me because of my other qualities, like brain power, good looks, stunning physique etc. but just because I told her she was beautiful?'

'Tony, you really are a good catch for any woman. You are kind, well-read, intelligent, and you have a well-paid job, good sense of humour as well as the fact that you would do

136

anything for anyone if they needed your help.'

'Well, let's just leave it that nothing happened and nothing is likely to happen with Bee. She's probably too young anyway, but it's a pity, she's been spoiled somehow. I sensed she had a brain, but she's hiding it behind this facade of commonness. She thinks it's great to work part-time stacking shelves and has no ambition.'

Maz gets up and goes to the kitchen area of the open-plan lounge, to start making coffee.

'We'd better have a coffee early, so that when the dog whines, the coffee will have had a chance to work its way through before the next walk,' she says without any pretence. She has it all worked out, probably remembering when she needed to go behind a tree and does not want to repeat the experience. 'It makes you wonder though, doesn't it, whether Bee's parents pushed her so hard to achieve that she took the other route?'

'Yeah, but can I be bothered to find out? She really was pretty awful and vulgar if you want the truth.'

'Going back to children being pushed too hard to achieve, I have seen it happen to others I've known. Sometimes the children become massively high-achievers, going on to university, getting first-class degrees then they end up cracking up, if it wasn't originally natural for them to be so academic. The parents, who pushed them, have to become carers for the rest of their lives. The adult children never become real adults, and never seem able to take responsibility, or to make decisions of their own. All the time the children are achieving highly at school, or at university, getting great grades, the parents are in their element, boasting to friends. Then crash, they can't understand what's happened.' She says, as she walks back from the kitchen area, with our coffee on a tray.

'Yeah Maz you could have a point, I suppose it is a possibility that she began to be pushed too hard because she mentioned her parents were power-tripping and argumentative.

137

All I can say is that they didn't achieve any goals with her. I wonder what they think of their failure?'

'Well we're just bouncing ideas around aren't we? It could be that none of that happened to Bee and somewhere along the line she inherited the type of genes for rebellion and you can't call her a 'failure' just because she doesn't live her life like you do.'

'Thanks Maz, I've never thought about this angle before, it's interesting. Perhaps it is what happened to her, the pushing bit, but then she got out of home and rebelled before she achieved anything.'

'She may be lucky that she did. Those pushy-type parents I was talking about end up employing psychologists, cognitive behavioural therapists, and no-one can get to the root of the problem because the high-achiever is not co-operative. They usually don't want to put any blame on their forceful parents because they have been brought up to be 'good'. Ah well, such is life, but perhaps it is worth having a think in relation to Bee.'

'I think I'll move on and put that down to bad experience. I can't be arsed to be someone's free analyst.'

'There'll be the right woman out there for you Tony. It will happen when you least expect it.'

'It's got so bad I've thought of using Internet dating, and Cheddar said I should see a prostitute. He can't understand my lack of pulling power, when he seems to be able to manage to squeeze a date out of anyone he takes a fancy to.'

'I don't believe you need the dating sites they are a dangerous waste of time. Certainly not a prostitute either. If you were to then meet a nice girl, you would feel really bad that in the back of your mind you knew you had that secret life, not only that, it might become addictive. I would like to see better for you. Just smile and be friendly to everyone.'

On the glass coffee table, my Android starts leaping about, vibrating. I see the caller is Bee and I have a momentary dilemma of whether to answer it or not. These new Androids are quite fun to work with, you can send emails, get on to Facebook, add a photo to your contacts, surf the net, get on to a thing called 'Maps' and add contacts so you can see where they are at any given time, unless they have hidden their location from you. I hid my location before I came here. I didn't want my contacts knowing that I am in Huddersfield, because I rather like the element of mystery in my disappearance for a few days. I am off the radar so to speak, so no Facebook, Twitter or emails but I did leave a note for my sister to tell her I was going away, in case she happened to notice the empty room.

'Watcha Bee, how ya doing?' I snatch the phone from the table at the last second.

'I wondered what was wrong with you, running out on me like that?' She says.

'It could be that you poured a drink into my lap, and I had already realised it just won't work between us, so I didn't see any point in prolonging the evening any further,' I reply, as I notice Maz get up and leave the room so feel freer to express myself. 'I was a bit shocked at your assumption I was going to sleep with you on the first night to be honest.'

'I thought that's all you blokes want.'

'Perhaps I came across like that when you met me at the speed-dating. I like a laugh, I'm not religious, and don't have any problem with people who want to hit the sack the first night but it's not for me. I'll be honest, it was what I thought and hoped would happen but when I was with you, some automatic reaction against it kicked in.'

'So, are you saying you could fancy me but not the sex?'

'Yeah that about sums it up, I suppose,' I reply, knowing I should really give her at least a little reassurance but I can't be bothered.

'So you're a celibate then.'

'Hang on, hang on, no, no you've got it all wrong. I always fancy that I will have sex. I am as red-blooded as the next man, in fact I'm steaming. I simply came to the conclusion, during the evening, that one-night stands are not for me.'

'Can we meet again? I really like you Tony, you're different.' She seems to have a less harsh tone, and has a little pleading in her voice, which I like.

'Look, I'm helping an old mate out so I'm in Huddersfield at the moment, looking after a greyhound. He's called Mac, don't you just love that?' I am being deliberately evasive.

'Yeah sounds cool,' she replies.

'Are you on Skype? We could have a Skype to Skype talk over the Internet when I get back if you like,' I offer half-heartedly.

'No, I don't have it, sorry. I could cook for you though, to say sorry about the cider. How long are you there for?'

First a bit of pleading, then a bit of apology, I am beginning to enjoy this.

'A few days, and look, you come to mine. I share a house with my sister but she travels with her work so doesn't usually get back 'til late on a Friday night. I'll buy in a pizza, a week on Friday, for six thirty. Got that? A week on Friday. When we end this call I'll text you the address. Take a taxi and I'll get you a taxi home. Come as yourself.'

'What do you mean by that? Are you being an arsehole?'

'Bee, calm it. I'd like to meet the real you, without all the slap and attitude. Give me a chance to know you.'

'See you Friday week then. Cheers m'dears.' With that she is gone, leaving me with a cringing despair at her sign-off. The dog starts to whine.

CHAPTER TWENTY ONE

After an excellent night's sleep in which I didn't wake at all to use the double-entrance bathroom, I wash and dress as I can hear Maz and John downstairs.

'Morning Tony, you obviously slept well because you didn't get up to the whining of Mac at seven,' Maz jests as she prods my arm. 'We are having a bacon sandwich, so I'll do one for you too.' Actually I remember now, I did hear the whining at seven but turned over and ignored it. There was a gentle breeze in my room, a comfortable bed and a feeling of complete contentment, why would I disturb that? I think to myself.

'You're looking better,' I say to John.

'Yes, much better thank you but Maz took the dog out on her own,' he reprimands me. 'She has also looked on the internet and found things to do today which won't involve me in much walking so I will accompany you both. We're going on a steam train ride, and then we will take a drive to the town of Holmfirth where they filmed *Last of the Summer Wine*. It was my favourite programme in its hey day you know.' The image of old Jolly John sitting in a tattered armchair, laughing at the antics of Compo, Clegg and Foggy, while salivating over Nora Batty springs to mind. I suppose this will be a real treat of a day out to him but sounds like my idea of hideous. However, after considering the alternatives of walking round the streets of Huddersfield or sitting in with the dog, I decide to accept.

As we approach the steam railway, I can see that it is advertised on a billboard as a "Superb ride out through the picturesque Pennines", which entails a return journey of about an hour. While we wait in a little wooden shed for the train to arrive, I actually start to feel quite excited at the prospect of a relaxing journey. It is drizzling and overcast outside but the promised picturesque countryside should compensate for the weather.

We climb aboard the train, which is puffing out billows of smoke, and sit on uncomfortable wooden bench seats. It surprises me, in light of the glossy advertising about this being a "picturesque" journey, that we quickly enter a long tunnel of grey rock face. I can see a tiny glimpse of light way, way ahead of us, so know that we will emerge at some point in the distance but how long it will take I can't calculate. Meanwhile I try to get comfortable in the gloom. After some minutes we emerge from the darkness of the tunnel and it takes a few moments for my eyes to readjust. I look to my right, as there is high weed-strewn bank to my left, which is not at all picturesque. I can see fields scattered with burnt out bonfires, and as I scrutinize further, masses of crushed beer cans and plastic bags are close to the cinders. Along the remaining minutes of our scintillating outward journey, someone with a warped sense of humour has artistically hung dirty, torn sleeping bags from tree branches. I assume they are the discarded bedding of the bonfire-makers.

Although I want to claim compensation for gross misrepresentation, the ride itself is okay. On the way back along the same route, on which I know there is nothing interesting to see, the click clacking of the train wheels and a gentle breeze is making me feel sleepy and relaxed. I wonder what it is about gentle breezes and sleepiness, I think I will look up to see if it is a known aid to sleep, and possibly buy a fan when I get home. No-one on the train is speaking. They must be having the same drowsy sensations.

After the train ride, Maz drives us to Holmfirth, which on first sight does nothing for me. For a start, I was really too young to understand the humour in the television programme, which I was obliged to watch with my mum if I was in the same room at the time. Nora Batty's droopy, wrinkled stockings and hair rollers just didn't make me laugh, but it's weird how I can remember the names of the characters.

The town seems to consist of a number of stone cottages and a few tourist shops and I find myself slouching with boredom.

'Not getting your camera out today, Tony?' quips John.

'Will do, when I see something interesting, John,' I reply, making an effort not to sound too sarcastic. However, when I visit the public toilets, there is a strange revelation. Having visited several main towns in my life, like Reading, Watford and the city of Paris, I have never come across a needle disposal unit installed in a toilet cubicle. The sign above the unit literally requests that drug users dispose of their needles with care. So here we are in a sleepy little town in the middle of the Penines and I discover it could be the drugs capital of England.

What I have enjoyed about the trips I have been on in the past few months, are these strange little discoveries. I have started to look around me and notice things. Perhaps it's the beginning of my journey into writing. I have been keeping a daily journal, in my flash-looking notebook, just like old Dylan Thomas used to do. Maz and I have to travel home tomorrow and I find myself already mentally preparing for Bee's visit. I will sort out my room, put up the shelves I've been promising myself and get some new bed linen. She will be the first girl to have been to my place. I invited a few over the years but, for various spurious reasons, my invitations were declined.

CHAPTER TWENTY-TWO

It has been several weeks since the trip to Huddersfield and I expect you are wondering what happened with Bee and me? Before I tell you about her, I will tell you about the team-building trip we had to go on at work. Ha, now I can picture your face, you really don't want to know do you? You just want me to get on with the interesting bit about Bee and me. Well, I will keep it short. As I told you before, I can't stand the false jollity that sycophants put on during these trips – no wonder they call them 'jollies'. Everything is paid for, like a hostel, your food, drink and entertainment, but you have to be in company you'd rather leave at work. If you have to go on one, take it from me, it's best to approach it all with nonchalance, a shrug of the shoulders and do it. You don't have much choice really, especially if you work in a place like I do. At the last one, someone had the great idea that we should go quad-biking.

How sitting alone, on a quad-bike with a helmet on your head adds to the feeling of being part of a team I fail to quite comprehend. When we arrived at the wooden hut in Somerset for the great event, I read the blurb and found out that part of the package was the insurance value of £50,000 per person. It was the first time I had ever considered my own value as a human being. It made me feel so much better knowing I had such a price on my head, and wondered what kind of technical expert sits in an office making those kinds of decisions.

If I was to be seriously injured, it meant the equivalent of two years' pay. So in the eyes of an Insurance Underwriter while I was riding on the quad bike, I was worth a lot less than an Andy Warhol painting and more than a Stieff Bear. At the time, the bear analogy made me think of Maz. She has owned a stout little bear for 50 years (yes, okay she is 51 you finally found out). Anyway, when she told me her bear was a boy called 'Wendy', I thought that was really quite imaginative, a boy bear called Wendy. Unfortunately, she soon made me realise she actually didn't really have much imagination as a child. 'Once I could read, I named him after reading the tag on his foot which said he was made by a woman called Wendy Boston who lived in Wales,' she said.

We had exhaustive instruction on how to handle the quad-bikes and were advised that it was going to be a 'fantastic' day out. We would be going up hills, through woodland and over dirt jumps. We were also told we should expect to get a little wet and muddy. I was tripping with excitement, and if you believe that, then you haven't been paying attention. Once we were all in our protective clothing and goggles, it was finally time to rev our engines and set off. As I stretched out my heavily padded, under-length arms, to grab the handlebars, I remember thinking I must look like a Wendy Boston teddy bear dressed in leathers.

I kindly held back as long as possible in order to let most of my 'team' mates go ahead of me. With the vibration of the quad bike searing through my body, I made it to the first mud jump, which was just through a small patch of woodland. As instructed, in order to take the jump, I revved my engine hard. I took off, and remember feeling mildly euphoric as the bike was flying through the air. The next thing I remember was being carted off in an ambulance.

I spent the rest of the weekend in the local hospital 'under observation'. This meant that I stayed in bed as groups of nurses, who came and went on various shifts, observed me from their nurses' station, by occasionally peering over the top of the latest glossy magazine. There was one old guy on my ward, who kept getting out of bed and wandering around wearing only his backless gown. It was not a pleasant sight. His arse cheeks were dimpled so it looked like this part of his anatomy was giving a mocking grin every time he passed by. He also had a habit of unclipping the Doctor's notes off the end of the beds, and I was seriously worried he would swap them round and I'd end up being wheeled off for a body part removal. I woke in the middle of the second night and caught the old geezer getting ready to pee in to my shoes, which were neatly placed at the side of my bed. I shouted at him to 'piss off', and finally got the attention of a nurse who gently manoeuvred him to the toilet then back to his bed, before she returned to my bedside to rudely tell me to, 'Stop disturbing the peace'.

The other thing that has happened recently is that Maz has started seeing someone called Hugh. Apparently she met him in her local pub, and he is an educated gardener so he kind of took over from me in stimulating her brain.

The night it was agreed Bee was to visit me, I made a bit of an effort and went to Marks and Spencer's for two pizzas, some garlic bread, and a ready-washed salad that you tip straight out on to the plate. I got a bottle of good wine to compensate for what I anticipated would turn out to be a seriously bad evening. My sister was away so we had the place to ourselves. In preparation, I put a white cloth on the table, laid the cutlery neatly, lit a candle and made a playlist of subtle music for my ipod. Maz likes to play what she calls 'easy listening' when friends come round, but I couldn't quite bring myself to play Dylan so I chose romantic jazz clarinet and saxophone. I borrowed the CD and ripped it to the ipod.

Well, as it happens, it was lucky I had at least made this amount of effort because Bee turned up at the door looking amazing. Gone was the brassy blonde hair, it was a glossy shade of mid-brown with highlights. Gone was the makeup except a subtle lengthening of her eyelashes with mascara and her lips were painted with a light reddish gloss. Her skin was good and shone on her cheeks. Gone was the false brashness. I virtually fell in love right there and then.

I've been doing a lot of thinking lately, and realise I was critical of Bee for doing the very things I was doing myself. With my dope-smoking, porn use, and generally looking for ways to cause a bit of chaos, I was being an idiot. Having been given opportunity to go to Paris and then the Hay Literary Festival, I have been able to apply more logic, to my life and I am a great fan of logic. I have enjoyed seeing another perspective and meeting some genuine people who I aspire to. Bee has made the effort at a much younger age than I did.

That evening we sat opposite each other in the candlelight and talked.

'I listened to a song on You Tube, Tony. It was by this brilliant band called *Revenge of the Pheasants*, the song was all about taking off your make-up and showing the real person beneath.'

'What was it that made you apply it to your life?'

'It was called '*Hide From You*,' and it got me thinking, real philosophically, about the direction of my life and how I was hiding behind make-up and an image of what I thought it was to be an adult. I had been thinking I was great, doing everything my parents would disapprove of, but really taking a path to ruin. Plus I fancied you.'

She told me she had been thinking a lot and realised she wanted more out of life than living in a run-down flat, working part-time when she could get herself a full-time job. So she put herself on an evening course to train in beauty and massage, and started speaking as she was brought up to do. She said it had been easier to readopt her natural spoken voice than it was to keep up the pretence of the other voice.

After about three glasses of wine she complimented me in a way no-one has done before, she said that at first sight she had sensed a bond would be possible between us, despite my hideous tee-shirt. She said that when she had leaned over and touched my hand at the speed-dating, she felt electricity that she had not experienced before. During the course of the evening, she told me all about the life she had led since leaving home, the various men she had slept with and I took it all in my stride. After all, that was the old 'fake' Bee. As she spoke, I felt the right stirrings in the crucial places but decided, that in my turn, I would wait and show her the respect that she deserved and had never yet experienced. I called her a taxi at eleven, and when I anticipated that she had arrived home I telephoned her as a gentleman would, to tell her what a pleasant evening it had been. The next day I even sent her a bunch of flowers by Interflora. Man, I felt happy in that moment with the person I've chosen to be.

Although things have been going pretty well in the love department, it can be a bit of a strain being the perfect gentleman, so she's had to get used to the odd fart or two. Maz and her new man, whom I have nicknamed Hog, on account of him being Hugh the Organic Gardener, have invited me for a meal next week. I haven't met him yet, as he has been hogging her attention for the last few weeks. I will try to keep an open mind, and attempt to avoid thinking, or talking about, hogs and anything they can be associated with.

The End

5269340R00083

Printed in Great Britain
by Amazon.co.uk, Ltd.,
Marston Gate.